Editor's Note: *Onward and Upward*

By Shaun Kilgore

ELCOME BACK, GANG. MYTHIC #19 marks our second monthly-occuring issue. I'm happy to report that the Kickstarter subscription drive did very well and a number of subscribers were added. In the same timeframe, MYTHIC's Patreon page has added several patrons to bring up the monthly total of our support. Between them both, I've had a quite a response. I want to thank everyone.

Since I'd like to reiterated that we are also offering advertisement space for science fiction and fantasy related projects. The rates are included in each issue. Plus, one of the perks of being published as a writer in MYTHIC is that you get ad space for your project which will appear in an issue of the magazine.

I want to repeat what I said in the previous Editor's Note. Here. I'll quote it:

> I'm still ironing out all of the details of this format change for **MYTHIC**. There is a subscription drive going on and a planned Kickstarter will likely start before many of you will receive this issue. For those of you who've read print issues of the magazine since it was started, the biggest change will be the trim size of each paperback issue. Since deciding on monthly issues, I've made the decision to shrink it from the previous 7 x 10 inches to 5.5 x 8.5 inches (a digest size, more or less.)
>
> The frequency of issues and finanical factors have also influenced my decision to drop the number of stories to at least

4 originals, 2-3 reprints as well as occasional nonfiction features like articles, essays, and reviews. I'll probably experiment with other features as well and have even thought about a throwback feature in the form of *Letters to the Editor*. Who knows what might happen? I do know that overall you'll receive more fiction each year that happened with the quarterly publication schedule.

So, the work continues as I work to make MYTHIC even better. I hope all of you will join me on this journey. Our destination still remains centered on becoming a professional-paying market. It's quite a climb, but I'll end by saying, "Onward and upward!"

INTERESTED IN SUBMITTING YOUR STORIES TO MYTHIC?

MYTHIC is looking for diverse science fiction and fantasy stories. You can send your submissions to me at submissions@mythicmag.com. Visit **www.mythicmag.com** for more information and instructions on how to format your submissions emails.

If you have any others questions, you can use the contact form on the website.

LETTERS TO THE EDITOR

MYTHIC welcomes letters to the editor from our readers. We appreciate your comments on the contents this issue. We prefer throughtful and consise letters of 500 or words or less. However, this is not a hard limit. We look forward to hearing from you.

You can email letters to the editor at mythicmag@gmail.com.

Include 'Letters to Editor' in your subject line, your full name, city, and state (or country).

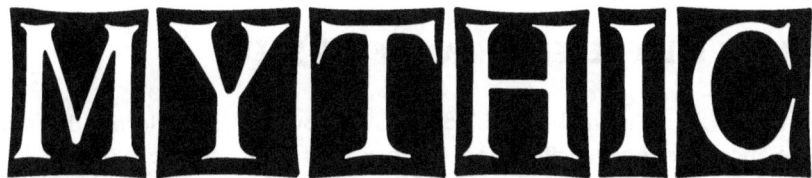

A SCIENCE FICTION & FANTASY MAGAZINE

ISSUE 19   FEBRUARY 2022

SHAUN KILGORE, EDITOR AND PUBLISHER

MYTHIC is a monthly publication. We publish speculative fiction, specifically science fiction and fantasy. Our mission is to expand the range of what is currently possible within both genres. We like new perspectives and new spins on familiar tropes. Diversity is a hallmark of our vision.

FOR SUBSCRIPTIONS VISIT OUR WEBSITE WWW.MYTHICMAG.COM.

MYTHIC #19: FEBRUARY 2022

ISBN: 978-1-945810-66-4

www.mythicmag.com
www.foundershousepublishing.com

Our Patrons

Here's where I take the opporunity to share a list of our current Patrons on Patreon:

Lin Faloon, Steven K. Smith, Marilyn J. Andrews, Dean Smith, Aaron Emmel, Brett Carlson, John Conner, Aaron Van Zile, Chris Jarvie, Ethan Guthrie Herrell, Heather Barden, Franklin L Kuzenski, Mary Jo Rabe, Andrew Kozma, Joanna Hoyt, Dina Leacock, Donna J. W. Munro, Buddy Hernandez, Kim Guymon, Alicia Caples, Antonis Triantafyllakis, Fábián Tamás, Ashton Moreland, Tom Jolly, Ian Chung, James Rumpel, Jonathan D Eaton, Randell Pinegar, Matt McNeill, Jonathan Hodge, Isabel Kunkle, David England, and Matt Hopper.

Consider joining these fine folks: Become A Patron Today!

If you haven't yet, please consider subscribing by becoming a Patron through **MYTHIC's Patreon Page**. Visit this address for more information: **www.patreon.com/mythicmag**. There are multiple ways to get monthly subscriptions. Help me keep MYTHIC going strong and growing into a top short fiction market.

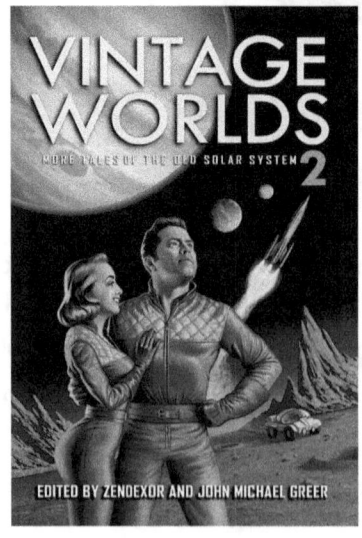

The Independent

By Sidney Blaylock Jr.

For my Grandmother, Katharyn Sparkman

S IENABAR SYSTEM. NORMALLY, it was considered a backwater system on the outskirts of the galaxy. However, as Ryn pulled up in a parking orbit far outside the station's normal traffic queue, she beheld a sight she'd never seen before. Ships of every description and type were clustered in various groups all around the station.

An incoming station alert broke her concentration. With a deft flick of her coconut-brown hand, she switched over from comms and brought up the alert on the display, expecting it to contain her berth number and unloading time.

The alert flashed red and blinked violently. Station closed.

Major gravitational anomalies detected. All ships are to assume a holding pattern—no exceptions. Any approaching ship will be considered hostile and will be fired upon immediately. Message repeats . . .

The message cycled again. Station closed? She'd never once seen a station closed for any reason. And gravitational anomalies? What did that even mean?

Suddenly, a collision alert warbled. Another ship, apparently fed up with waiting, had decided to vector back to Sienabar—right through her designated flight path. No time for subtlety—she grabbed the manual flight controls and threw the ship into a violent burn "down-relative" to the other ship.

Even though there was no "up" or "down" in space, her brain still compared everything to that coordinate system—which was probably why she was a far better pilot than her father.

The Independent's defensive screens flared briefly as they came in contact with the screens of the other ship, but there was no damage done.

Ryn slumped back into the rough padding of her seat as a comm burst from the other ship slammed into her queue. She deleted it without even listening.

"Ryn!" her father barked.

"Not my fault!" she yelled back. "Station's closed. They've corralled us into a holding pattern. Other ships are going back down to the planet—through us, apparently."

His voice lowered an octave . . . not a good sign. "Well, we can kiss our on-time bonus goodbye." She could almost envision him shaking his head. "Unbelievable."

"When are you coming up?"

"I'm not. I've still got to prep this loader for sale. Unless you'd rather not eat while we're station side?"

"But—"

"But nothing," he interrupted, "you're Captain. The ship's yours today."

She shook her head and felt the dreadlocks on her tickle the nape of her neck. "What if there's an emergency?"

He sighed. "If you need me, just call out. I don't want to die out here any more than you do. Remember—it's Rule One out here." He cut the comms, but not before she heard swearing as he struggled to shift the loader into the appropriate bay for unloading at the station once they docked at the station—whenever that would be.

Rule One. *Stay alive, whatever it takes.* Suddenly, everything felt less safe.

Ryn moved to put the ship on a more vigilant footing. While it would mean a little more in terms of power expenditure, the gain in situational awareness would more than offset the additional power drain. She flipped her scans over to active from passive and dialed up the defensive screens. However, Ryn felt that it was the scan that really would yield the most results. Her ship began to actively ping the various ships in her local queue, querying their IDs and comparing the returned information, sorting through discrepancies, and marking ships based on distance, type, and perceived threat.

Ryn eased back in the captain's chair, then snapped upright when a yellow marker flipped to red indicating a weapons lock on *The Independent*. She skimmed the scan, looking for the ship's ID stats—*Vesper Star*. She requested removal, but was auto-denied. She requested adjudication—and was again denied. The weapons lock remained.

Grinding her teeth, she brought up external comms. The system connected to the offending ship and compensated for lag.

"*Vesper Star*, this is IND-1145, identifying as *The Independent*. You've got a weapons lock on us. Stand down, I repeat stand down. I have taken no hostile action against you and do not have you on weapons lock."

A reply came after a few moments lag.

"Check your protocols, IND-1145. We are a Queenship."

The reply came from a female voice that seemed devoid of emotion. The other captain cut comms as if that explained everything.

Ryn brought up her scan again and cycled through the ships' listings until she found the *Vesper Star*. She flicked through the stats and saw that the *Vesper Star* was indeed listed as a Queenship. She tapped on the holographic display to read more. Much like an embassy, Queenships were considered sovereign territory. Her mouth dropped and she immediately keyed in an exception and overrode active scan on *Vesper Star*. Essentially, in painting all ships in the area as potential hostiles, she had effectively (and quite unintentionally) declared hostile intentions toward a sovereign state—an action that in some systems, the profile helpfully supplied, meant that she had effectively declared war on the Queen-in-Residence on *Vesper Star*.

However, taking *Vesper Star* off active scan wasn't without risk, however. It meant that she had to trust the other ship completely—it could blow her away without registering as a threat on her boards. Still, she had no intention of declaring war on anyone, especially not a Queenship five or six times *The Independent's* mass.

"Sorry about that, *Vesper Star*," Ryn said, glad that her brown skin hid the rising flush on her face. "I didn't realize you had a different protocol profile."

The Independent's scan beeped and went back to yellow, indicating that the weapons lock had been cleared.

"Now you do," the other captain's voice replied. While still cool, and seemingly unnaturally calm, there was a thaw to it. "Is this your first time in the Captain's chair?"

"No," she said, knowing that the question wasn't meant to cut, but feeling the bleeding edge of it nonetheless. "But it's my father's ship," she felt compelled to add. "He keeps putting me the Captain's chair."

"That's the nature of parents. I think parents have this notion that throwing their kids out into the void will . . . help . . . them . . . ."

The other Captain trailed off as if distracted. Suddenly, chatter spiked, both on the *Vesper Star* and also on her own external comms. Other ships' engines were spooling up and they were beginning to boost out on wildly chaotic vectors.

Ryn felt her heart begin to hammer. She checked her displays and scans, but except for everyone careening wildly, everything still showed as normal. "*Vesper Star*, you're seeing this, right? Do you know what's going on? I don't see anything."

There was a delay that was far longer than simple lag. "Something's coming in about the station--some of the ships closer in are saying that it's been blown. Not getting a confirmation . . . but they all keep screaming about ships warping in. Varda, clean up these scans." Ryn heard an affirmative from the other captain's crew member.

Ryn frantically reviewed her scans, but, like *Vesper Star*, all she was getting was a cloudy mess intermittently broken up by ships darting away on all vectors. She looked at the Egress Point opened by the station—a huge gaping hole of darkness that cost way more money to use than she or her father had at the moment. Why would they open it, she wondered, but then she saw the escape pods ejecting *en masse* from the station. She was just about to switch to internal comms and bring her dad in on all this when a bright light flared for a moment and then faded back into darkness. The station's icon disappeared from her scans.

However, that wasn't the most terrifying thing that Ryn saw. In front of her, space seemed to . . . elongate . . . as if being stretched to infinity. This stretching was nothing like the gravitational lensing effect that she saw around black holes and super massive objects. No, this lensing was different, almost as if it stretched to infinity as if both light and space had suddenly been given extra depth. Something emerged. She wasn't sure if she could call it a ship as it was twisted and curled. It clearly wasn't organic, but somehow it seemed move and shift, swirling in on itself.

Suddenly, there was a cacophony over the comms as more and more of the swirling ships—*swirls*, as she thought of them—poured out through those strange, elongated frame-dragging funnels.

Liquid, curling streams of some unknown energy erupted again and again from them, blazing silently in the darkness. Ships who hadn't taken precautions exploded silently and serenely under the intense fire. Ships that had taken precautions saw their defensive screens light up as those screens took the brunt of the assault. Shouts and screams over the comms assaulted Ryn as the terrified and the horrified merged with the injured and the dying. While the vacuum of space was cold, silent, and unyielding, the tumult of those who fought to cling to life was anything but that.

A frantic beeping alerted Ryn. While the swirls had started emerging near the station, they had begun appearing further and further out. They were now entering the edge of her local cluster. One emerged just out of *The Independent's* weapon range, but well within *Vesper Star's* range. One of *Vesper Star's* cannons deftly tracked the swirling ship's movement and opened fire. The first volley cracked its apparently weak shielding and the second volley split it into a cascade of debris. While there was no explosion, an ever expanding cluster of fragments warped space and seemed to drag the whole fabric of space-time along with it as it moved like particles dragged along in the current of a fast moving river.

Her comm unit pinged.

"The station opened the Egress Point before it was blown," *Vesper Star's* captain called out over the cacophony, "head for it and we'll cover you out-system!"

Even now, that ship's massive engines were flaring, as it slowly built inertia. Soon, with both its mass and guns, it would be a juggernaut and nearly impossible to stop.

"We don't have the funds! It'll never let us through." Even in the midst of this crisis, heat rose in her cheeks at having to admit this, especially another ship's captain. She gulped as the enormity of what she had just said hit her like nova exploding.

She and her father were trapped.

The other captain's response was immediate. "We'll spot you—now move!"

Ryn slammed her own engines in response. *The Independent*, while a much smaller ship, and boasting smaller engines, was still carrying much less mass, even under a full load hauling the power loader, than the Queenship.

Ryn's internal comms lit up and she heard her father cursing in her ears. "I told you about that!" he yelled, apparently still unaware of the chaos all around. "I still haven't gotten this loader hooked in—no more cowboy maneuvers!"

Her heart thundering, she keyed over to his comm unit. "They've blown the station!"

Her gaze darting over the increasingly hostile vacuum of space. "They're swarming all over us. We're going to get killed if we stay here! The Queenship said that the Egress Point is open and to burn for it!"

"The station's blown? What Queenship and who's swarming? Pirates?"

Ryn loved her father, but she had no time for this. Even now, *The Independent* was screaming at her to acknowledge half a dozen warnings. He needed to be in this chair right now--flying this ship, making these decisions.

But he wasn't.

She was.

"Dad, get that thing stowed and get up here!" she called out and then cut the comms. With savage swipes, she acknowledged several warnings in quick succession, gripped the manual controls, and settled deeper into the captain's chair, letting the information wash over her.

A cluster of the swirl ships had apparently seen their group and were vectoring in towards them. Towards the *Vesper Star*, she thought as they rocketed in. While it was far from the largest ship in their queue, *Vesper Star's* guns bristled and the Queenship had already managed to pop the hulls of several of the twisting craft that entered in range of its formidable guns.

She wished her father would hurry up—she was the better flyer, as her reflexes were far sharper, but she could really use his wisdom right about now, and she knew she could draw on the support of him just being there—if he would just get up here.

Her initial burn had put her ahead of *Vesper Star*, but its massive engines were finally doing the job of moving the more massive ship. Soon it would pass her and then she would be the one falling behind.

Now all she thought about was escape. When was her father going to finish locking that loader down?

Before she could ping his comm unit again, a swirl ship emerged almost right on top of her.

Rule One.

Without thinking, she repeated her dodging maneuver from earlier, spinning the ship "down" relative to the strange swirling ship. *The Independent* twisted away, but it wasn't quite far enough. Somehow, she slid into the elongated space where the swirl had emerged. She felt a ripple throughout her body if she had just crossed some sort of threshold. Then it was as if all of reality had just ceased to exist . . . and that's when everything stopped making sense.

She screamed in pain. Her body all of a sudden wrenched in several different directions. Only her hold on the controls kept her from grasping at her body and curling in a fetal position. It was if she had stomach cramps, arthritis, sinusitis and a migraine all at the same time. Her bones, while not broken, felt as if they were twisting and morphing all through her body. As she struggled to fly the ship, *The Independent* wasn't in much better shape itself. Warnings, sirens, and claxons screamed for attention as pretty much every system was pushed to, or in some cases, past their tolerances. Luckily, life support stayed up and she still had flight controls, but several areas midship had already buckled, and several others were on the verge of structural failure.

She struggled to keep the ship steady, fighting through the pain even as tears slid down her cheek. Gritting her teeth, and hanging on for dear life despite the pain, she beheld the chaos in her view-screen. The stars were still around her, but they were strange. Their light seemed to be a continuum--that stretched all the way to infinity. Space itself had constricted to a curved tunnel through which everything seemed to move. The space-time that she was used to was all around her, but seemed to be *sliced* into chunks that slid past her one after the other. It was almost as if she were watching *time* itself happening in one discrete instant, one after the other.

Every chunk that passed seemed to inform the next chunk. It was almost as if she could see time in slices. The past informed the future in that it was almost as if she could see the future coalescing in front of her. Her present seemed assembled from her past and the future seemed to be possibilities *merging* into one possible present.

All of a sudden, the image of an ant from Earth crawling on the outside of a wire flashed into her memory. The teaching AI had been explaining the concept of extra dimensions and how they might be coiled up around space-time, existing all around, but effectively locked away and not discernible by the ants on the outside of the coil, much less something that the ant could interacted with.

Were humans really ants, crawling on the outside of space-time, while these—whatever they were—lived in this coiled time-space? She stared at the incredible seen before her and wondered if it was possible for those who evolved here to see time, or even more strangely, to see the future, and the past, as easily as she looked at a scan and saw the present?

Ryn didn't know for sure, but it sure seemed like it based

on the way her twisted body was laboring. She even struggled to breathe as it was hard for her lungs to inhale air and breathing was shallow. She was lightheaded, and it seemed to be getting worse.

The time slices seemed to be resolving themselves and becoming clearer. Yes, there! "Up" relative to her was a swirl that would be transitioning back into her space—her space-time rippled ahead like water in the myriad of lakes planet-side—and she sent *The Independent* hurtling towards it. Systems screamed in protest and the ship lurched as several internal supports failed. She shivered at each vibration, expecting it to be her last. When she hit the barrier, the stars elongated and then shifted back to normal stars. She was back in real space—her space-time!

Her external comms pinged. The captain of *Vesper Star's* voice sounded in her ears like a supernova explosion. "*Independent*, we thought we'd lost you! We're boosting towards the Egress Point now—the system's primed for you too."

Ryn looked up and was shocked to see that *Vesper Star* was almost at the Egress Point. In fact, the ship was just beginning to reach the acceleration node and would be gone in a matter of minutes. Swirls still swarmed all around.

"We'll give you covering fire from our aft guns, but we can't stay. The Queen's safety is my first duty."

Already overtaxed, her brain felt like it was going to explode.

Over the comms, she heard a scraping, a loud thump, and then something slammed into the inner hull, and her ship shuddered. There was an ominous metallic screech and a liquid squelching sound. The ship suddenly felt off-center and ungainly.

Ryn's stomach roiled. In trying to save the ship in the other dimension, she'd forgotten all about her father.

"Daddy!" she screamed. No response.

She screamed for him again, but nothing. Her scans flashed at her, commanding her attention. A swirl-ship had lined her up and fired. Screeches erupted from the defensive screens in protest. She launched her last set of countermeasures—her offensive pods. The ship's last two automated drones zipped out of blister pods and swept around *The Independent* to augment the ship's minimal firepower with their own targeting systems and autonomous weapons.

Ryn needed to get down to the hold and check on her father, but the screens continued to protest under the withering fire of the swirl. His non-responsiveness and the sluggishness of the ship told her everything she needed to know. Either he hadn't gotten the loader fully strapped down and either it had crushed him, or he had been crushed and broken in the other dimension. Her body still ached in places from the effects of the other space, and she had been strapped in.

A tiny part of her hoped he might still be alive, even though, rationally, she knew that was probably impossible. Even if he had survived being crushed by the loader, the G-forces of all her maneuvers would have reduced his bones to powder by now.

Her main problem now was that she couldn't maneuver. The free-floating loader made the ship far too sluggish as it bounded off the weakened inner hull—which was another worry. If the frame buckled, she'd lose engines. And if she lost her engines, then she was as good a dead.

There was only one thing she could do, but her finger hovered over the cargo bay release. If her father wasn't dead, then she would kill him by condemning him to be sucked out by the unforgiving vacuum of space.

The defensive screen began to flicker. It was going to fail—and she was going to die.

Rule One, her father's voice echoed in her mind.

With an internal scream that seemed more infinite than

the universe itself, she stabbed release. The sound of air whooshed out over the comms and apparently the loader did as well as suddenly her controls responded instantly to her commands once more.

Snapping *The Independent* over, she rolled the craft onto its underside and brought up the relatively fresh defensive screen just as the damaged one flickered out.

There was no exultation, however.

Ryn felt a bone-numbing weariness that seemed to seep down into her core.

Her comms lit up one final time.

"Your account is primed and the Egress Point's set, *Independent.* Hit the Egress and we'll meet up in Sairose system. I'll see you on the other side." The captain gave a command to her crew and then *Vesper Star* was gone.

Alone.

Ryn's mouth went dry. She was going to die here. She could only stare at the receding glare of the *Vesper Star's* engines as it accelerated away. Wrecked husks of blown freighters, tankers, and the myriad of other ships unfortunate enough to be in-system today were all that were left. That and the swirls.

Even as she watched, she could see her window of opportunity closing. Swirls were beginning to swarm the gap between her and the Egress Point. There was no chance she could make it.

Almost no chance. She could overpower her engines.

It could work, but there was a problem. She would need to bleed power from another system, and the only ones with enough juice right now were the weapons, the screens, or life support. So she could either be weaponless, defenseless or she could suffocate. And heaven help her if she overloaded the engines. While she could maneuver on thrusters alone, they wouldn't cut it against the swirl-ships.

There was a dull ache, almost a physical pain, in Ryn's core. She wanted to ask her father what to do. But there was no one—just her, in a life or death situation that was looking more grim by the moment. It was either weapons or screens!

Praying that a good offense was better than a bad defense, she overrode the safeties and channelled power from the defense screens into her engines. The G-force slammed her back into the captain's chair as *The Independent* surged forward.

Something inside her wanted to face death with her eyes open—she knew that with her screens down, her hull was all that stood between her and death. One shot, even an errant one, in the right place, would finish her. A part of her wished that it would happen, that she could see the enveloping darkness and in that one terrifying moment, she felt she would feel her father's arms encompass her. Another part of her screamed in rebellion, terrified of the darkness that would claim her, and it fought, storming up through her. It was if her body moved on its own accord. It wanted to live.

Suddenly, the curious bifurcation of herself was gone and she knew what she wanted with all her heart.

I want to live!

Even though swirls were making runs at her at an alarming rate, she could do this—no, she *would* do this! The engines roared ever louder, taking in more and more power as Ryn slowly bleed the screens dry. Swirls were vectoring in from all sides, but although her heart thudded in her chest, she kept her breaths short and quick. She rolled the ship, she dodged and feinted. She couldn't let the engines burn for too much longer or she was going to have too much velocity for her thrusters to line her up for the Egress Point and she'd overshoot it.

Four swirls vectored in and she wrangled the controls. One of her offensive pods blew the first ship, while the second pod tore whatever those things were using for engines off another as its mangled carcass went careening past.

She was almost there, having closed most of the distance to the Egress Point in that one titanic burst. She hit her thrusters and slammed forward as the ship slowed and rolled, lining her up for the first acceleration node of the Egress Point. Two more swirls came charging in. One fired a shot that flared like a nova. Ryn half-screamed. She thought that it had slipped past her depleted screens and that her life was over, but realized that it had just slid off the side of the cockpit. As the swirl slid past, she commanded her pods to make it their highest priority and stabbed her own fire controls again and again letting a guttural yell. Under the combined fire of the pods and her weapons, the swirl exploded into fragments.

Her ship rocked. Again, sure that she'd been hit, an involuntary breath escaped Ryn when she saw that it was one of the two pods flaring into nothingness. Now only one pod remained, zipping around her ship, firing bursts at any swirl unfortunate enough to come in range.

Ryn wiped the sweat from her eye to make sure she aligned up her ship with pulsating darkness. Alarms were nearly continuous now.

She gunned *The Independent's* engines and was slammed back into her seat. She sped through node after node, gaining speed, but paradoxically, time seemed to slow, then all went black and suddenly, she could see again.

The ship's interior looked like always had, but now the stars were gone. There was nothing but blackness outside, indicating the ship's smooth integration into the Egress Point. Now she was pulled ahead by the steady, comfortable pull of the powerful, but expensive, gravitational generators.

Ryn said a silent thank you to the still nameless captain of *Vesper Star*. She had no idea what awaited her ahead when she returned to normal space, but for now, at least, she was safe.

The alarms fell blissfully silent.

However, after a moment, Ryn almost wished for the blaring alarms again. Although safe, *The Independent* was now as silent as a grave, and she wept for it.

About the Author

SIDNEY BLAYLOCK, JR. grew up and currently lives in Chattanooga, Tennessee and has worked as a Bookseller, Library Assistant, Adjunct Instructor, and 6th Grade Language Arts Teacher. Sidney is currently a Visiting Scholar of African American Literature at Jacksonville State University. In addition, he is currently pursuing his PhD at Middle Tennessee State University where he is working on his dissertation dealing with Rhetoric, Film, and Afrofuturism.

A lifelong lover of Science Fiction and Fantasy in all its forms, Sidney's most recent publications include "HawkeMoon" which was selected Cover Story for *Storyhack*, Issue 4 (August 2019) and "Skin Deep," (February 2017) published on *Aurora Wolf* (aurorawolf.com). Other publications include stories in: Electric Spec (electricspec.com), *Visions VI: Galaxies, Visions IV: The Space Between Stars, Fae,* and *Tales of the Talisman.* Additionally, Sidney's story in *Fae* ("Faerie Knight") was a starred story on the Tangent Recommended Reading List for 2014.

Sidney discusses writing, film, and technology and video games on his personal blog at https://sidneyblaylockjr.wordpress. com.

Far from Twilight

By D. A. D'Amico

THE FOREST DIDN'T quite have the energy to kill her in the perpetual night this far from twilight. Soji frowned as she stomped back the grasping cluster of coin-shaped black leaves working its way up the fur lined ankle of her left boot, and braced herself for a much quicker end as a silver caudal fin broke the icepack nearby.

She knelt, heart pounding, her breath mingling with the perpetual snow as she adjusted her goggles to enhance the bleak landscape. A meter away, the knife-edged fin vanished beneath a pyramidal mount of ebony-tinted fronds that swayed as the creature churned the ice below, severing the plant's buried insulation bladders, and releasing a sweet cherry-like odor into the frigid air.

"Don't be shy." She laughed humorlessly as she knelt to pat the greyish snow with one oversized glove. Above, a fat pinpoint of harsh bluish-white flared. One of the Three Sisters, the trio of stars that kept this world locked-in with one face always toward its primary sun. "I won't run."

As if running would do her any good. The creature's first pass was to break up the crust. Its second would bring the killer to the surface, and the monster could move a whole lot faster than she could in this dark and frigid wasteland.

It had been a different world ten years ago, mostly desert, a dying planet with a small colony of humans and extra-Terrans existing on the fringes of perpetual twilight. Then

Soji had come. To her credit, her intention had never been to land. It had taken ahuu weapons to force her ship into the atmosphere. Bad luck had crashed it, killing her crew and driving Soji to flee with her precious cargo.

That cargo, the genetic memory of another dying world, had been worth killing for. Soji should have let the ahuu take it. Then, at least, this world wouldn't have had to die. But she'd cared about her mission. She'd cared about a lot of things back then.

The fin reappeared twenty meters away in a low cluster of cobalt-colored fronds that waved languidly in the stiff wind like deep sea creatures. It circled once, churning up the ice before breaching the surface in a cloud of pinkish snow crystals.

Then it charged.

"It's about time." She told herself she wanted this. It was a fitting end to a messed-up story. It was time the planet made her pay for her sins.

Blunt barbs along its silvered belly flexed. A wide, circular maw opened, and four meters of armored, segmented muscle propelled the teardrop-shaped monster rapidly across the uneven snowpack.

Soji tensed. She held her ground as the creature rushed closer. At ten meters, she could hear the trilling squeal of its fat tongue gliding across rows of jagged teeth. At five, she could smell the sickly cloying odor of cinnamon and cloves, a unique mixture she'd learned to associate with this world, and probably the last thing she'd ever smell.

It moved so fast she barely had time to close her eyes before it was on her in a rush of hot air, crushing her into the burning-cold snow, shredding her light weatherproof armor. Needle sharp teeth tore into her right arm. She smelled blood, felt the blast of supercooled air inside her suit turning her sweat to ice.

She screamed. A sharp twang split the noise. The monster's bulk heaved, shuddered, and went still.

Soft words broke the crash of her frenzied breathing, nearly missed, hidden among her choked gasps and agonized whimpers. "We need to speak."

Her body ached. Her skin burned with the onset of frostbite where the monster had ripped its way through her armor, and real fear had replaced her languid depression. She'd come too close this time.

The voice returned, louder, more insistent. "Human Soji. We must speak."

Soji felt it at the back of her neck, an intrusion on the uppermost layer of her thoughts. She flexed her muscles. Her right arm slid free from a spike of bone, and she cried.

"Who?" She croaked as she tugged herself from the limp, bifurcated lobe of the iceworm's mouth and into the startlingly bright and frigid air.

"Have you forgotten me, old enemy?"

Soji grunted. "Iex?"

The tattered collar of her suit hissed. The pain subsided, leaving only the cold and the uneasy sensation of dead flesh being dragged across her body as the armor repaired itself.

"Get me out of here." She twisted under the worm. Her armor could fix itself, but it couldn't lift a twelve-ton behemoth off her chest.

She sensed movement outside the range of her vision. The pressure nailing her to the ground relaxed, and her breath wheezed out in a sigh. Something metallic grasped her right foot. It yanked her out into the full night, leaving her winded and stunned.

"Iex?" She hadn't seen the ahuu in over a year, not since it had tried to have her extradited to her home world of Chambria. It had been the first time he hadn't actually tried to kill her in almost a decade.

"I'm glad I have found you like this." The ahuu's voice sounded harsh, with a slight lisp, as if the dented and worn translator hanging from the creature's neck had trouble processing the syntax.

"I bet you are," Soji said as she heaved herself slowly to her feet. She felt lightheaded, her body stiff, but alive.

The bulk of the iceworm loomed behind her in the false light of her goggles, a mountainous glob of muscle and spikes. A meter long shaft of violet-colored metal protruded from the pebbled sensory bundle along its crest, and thick blue-black tendrils of vegetation had already begun to swallowed it. Even this far from twilight, the jungle could find the energy to feed.

"I heard you were on the planet again," she said.

"Only for the briefest of times." The ahuu's bulbous black head, sleek, seal-like, and featureless except for two yellow pinpoint eyes, dipped slightly in her direction.

His neck sagged nearly to his waist, sloping across low hanging shoulders to stick-like arms. Long fat fingers like stubby tentacles had been attached to those arms the first time Soji had seen the creature. Now, they ended in charred-looking stumps, caused by the native sapient creatures on this world, but indirectly her doing.

A delicate cage-like structure of copper-colored slats sat against the ahuu's steeply sloping shoulders and wound in helix-like curves along his arms. Where his hands should have been, dark green prosthetic fingers hung like ripe jalapenos, curled and grasping a white-plastic weapon that resembled a crossbow.

"So, this is how it ends?" Had Iex saved her from the worm so he could murder her himself? There was some poetry to it, she supposed. If the ahuu had killed her when she'd crashed on this world a decade ago, it might have saved a doomed race.

"It ends in eleven standard hours," the ahuu said. "The

last ship leaves this world, and I will be on it. Will you?"

She frowned. "Are you going to kill me, or not?"

The creature trilled. "Kill you? I *need* you."

I T'S TIME." THE ahuu slouched through the airlock of the small capsule with Soji in tow. "You cannot hope to retrieve it on your own, and you dare not leave it."

Soji tiptoed warily through drifts of peach-colored pebbled glass scattered across the decking in the first compartment. They had no function as far as she knew, and she'd never bothered to ask.

The inner section held two stiff resin seats tailored with spongy silver brackets fit for an average humanoid form, and its pale blue walls were covered with triangular notches that seemed to swallow stray sound, pulling the words from her lips as she spoke.

"I don't know what you're talking about, Iex," she mumbled.

The ahuu spun. Emotionless specs of watery yellow peered deeply into her eyes, never blinking. Soji didn't even know if he *could* blink.

"The memory block," Iex said slowly, his translator laboring over every syllable. "The matrix containing the genetic knowledge of Cerberus 3B. You knew where it was once. You can find it again."

Of course, she could find it. She'd given it to the nintti ten years ago when she'd crashed here on her way to Earth, and it'd been the catalyst of catastrophe. How could she unleash that on another planet?

"You're crazy!" She yelled.

"My mind is on straight!" The translator barked back.

The cage around the ahuu's arms swiveled. A jumble of prosthetics flew up, and for a moment Soji thought he might hit her. Then he tumbled into the nearest seat.

"The colony is dissolving. Every one of the sapient races is abandoning this world," he said. The worn translator seemed to soften his tones, finally getting the hang of the ahuu's speech. "It is my last chance at redemption. It could be yours as well."

She thought about that. The ahuu's idea of redemption was to complete a decade old mission; obtain the matrix for his herd.

Soji was beyond redemption.

W E'VE HAD THIS discussion a hundred times, Iex," she said as she rubbed her temples. Her shoulder ached, but her suit doctor had been busy repairing the damage from the iceworm. "It's better off on this world."

"Better off now that it has already killed this planet?" The ahuu's words tasted red, sarcastic and salty.

Soji jumped to her feet, breathless and shaking. The transit synesthesia was startling, brief, and all too familiar. He'd launched the capsule with her on board.

"Show me!" She screamed.

The top of the ship melted away in rivulets and runnels like hot mercury being poured over a clear glass cap. The stars became visible. The big yellow primary glared like a jaundiced eye above, almost obscuring one of the pair of harsh bluish sister suns that sat like a mote in its corner.

The world spread out below like a tarnished coin, blistering gold at one end, dusky black at the other. A band of brilliant green surrounded its center like a jade ring, trailing streamers in shades of emerald and topaz toward the sunbaked side. Tendrils of sapphire, amethyst, and obsidian seemed to ooze down into the near-absolute blackness of the shrouded pole where a cluster of silver splotches shone like misplaced stars.

"You had no right!" It was the first time she'd been off planet since the catastrophe. She'd sworn never to leave, and he'd tricked her.

The ahuu swiveled its head in her direction, pinning her with the gaze from its intense yellow eyes. "Tell me what I ask, and you may return. If not…"

The view outside altered. The silver splotches grew, revealing the outlines of massive starships, their tapered cylindrical hulls marked with the indents of hundreds of docking cradles.

Thin squeals echoed from the cabin walls. Soji's translator picked them up, regurgitating the unfamiliar language. "We near the completion of the forced exodus. Citizens of all species must comply…"

The craft shook. "It has us in its field now," Iex said. "In a few moments, we will be tethered and unable to break free. It is your choice?"

Soji swore. She couldn't leave, not now. Maybe not ever. "I know we've had a few scrapes in the past, Iex, but we're friends. This goes too far."

The ahuu tilted its head alarmingly, a sign of mirth. "We have tried to kill or to have each other deported, imprisoned, or enslaved on more occasions than I can recall. We are so much closer than just friends."

It was true. They'd had a cat and mouse relationship, or more closely, a spy vs spy relationship since Iex had tried to kill her over the matrix nearly a decade earlier. In return, Soji'd given him to the mercies of the nintti. From there, it had been one attempt after another on both their parts. This had gone on for so long they'd eventually developed a grudging respect for each other.

The squeal intensified. Orders barked out what sounded like jakaidian, and Soji realized she'd be subject to interstellar law once the ahuu had her aboard. Iex must have known she couldn't risk it. That's why he hadn't warned her when he'd taken off.

She held her breath as the final warning droned through

the button translator behind her left ear. Should she let the matrix off planet after she'd seen what it had done? Could the ahuu be trusted with that kind of power?

The shuttle jolted. "Magnetic lock in ten seconds. Your choice?"

"I can't." She bit her lip, watching hopelessly as the last of the planet vanished behind the looming bulk of the starship.

"Three... two..."

She couldn't let the ahuu have it. If he brought it home, his people might very well destroy their world the way the nintti had. She didn't hate him enough to let that happen.

"One."

"Okay!" She screamed. "Alright, you win."

ER THOUGHTS SWIRLED as quickly as the perpetual storms across the planet's night-day boundary. The shuttle had fallen rapidly into the planet's atmosphere, headed in a shallow arc from the cluster of starships to a destination deep in the verdant twilight zone.

"Did you think I wouldn't notice," she said softly. She'd felt the capsule disengage just before she'd agreed. Iex had no intention of taking her away.

The ahuu lifted his steeply sloping shoulders in a very human approximation of a shrug. "I couldn't risk getting trapped either. Time is short, and we desire the matrix as strongly as had the nintti."

"Look what happened to them," she snarled, amazed at the ahuu's ignorance.

The nintti had been the indigenous race on the planet before Soji had arrived. They'd lived along the twilight band, hidden from the harsh desert environment in extinct volcanic nodules, content in their own way. Then Soji had crashed, bringing the genetic matrix like the apple into the garden of Eden.

"The nintti were incautious," Iex replied, Soji's translator flatly repeating his shrill cries with none of the implied passion. "They did not fully understand the technology, and paid the price for their hubris."

"And you won't? Is that it?"

"No," he said with finality, and turned away as the jungle rushed up to meet them.

Is this a joke?" Iex used the shuttle's field emitters to crush a tunnel deep into the seething rainforest, and they dropped into the shaft, sinking slowly past a wall of branches that writhed and strained against the capsule's repressor field.

"No," Soji said flatly. "It's here, right where I left it."

"But this..." The translator's severe tones faded.

Soji nodded as they finally touched down. Outside, a crazy swarm of branches curled outward, reaching for the ship with wide gold-tinted leaves that flexed like grasping hands. Squat lizards with kangaroo-like flanks and azure plated scales hopped within the cluster, chittering like marmosets, squealing occasionally as spears of foliage pierced their thick hides and dragged them deeper into the impenetrable brush.

"This is where we crashed," she said. "Where you shot down my ship, and where my crew died. They're still out there under all... this."

The last words came out with more bitterness than she'd intended. The crash had happened a long time ago. She'd come to terms with her loss, as she'd come to understand the aloof ahuu. Neither would change no matter what happened in the next few hours.

The forest thinned momentarily, revealing a long scar in the bedrock beneath as if beckoning her to step outside. "We walk from here."

"Unlikely." Iex closed his small eyes in a gesture of disbelief.

Soji shrugged. "Then take us back up. I'm sure we still have a few hours until the fleet disperses."

She dropped into the chair, turning her back with a sarcastic smile.

The ahuu said something the translator wouldn't repeat.

YOU WILL DIE instantly if you step more than three meters from this device," Iex said as it strapped a long cylindrical rod to the cage around his upper body, twisting it until it emitted a dull orange glow.

"That's a bit of an exaggeration," she chuckled nervously. It was, but not by much.

The forest bent back around them. Branches groaned and snapped. A lizard squealed. Flying insects, vines with flailing blade-shaped leaves, and leathery seed pods with razor-sharp whirling edges bounced away, forced outward by the expanding field as the mobile emitter unfolded.

"It's not far," she said taking a deep breath. The air smelled like burnt cinnamon.

"Best if it is not." Iex hefted the bone-colored crossbow in his prosthetic hands, cradling it in long green fingers. It might only be a coincidence that it was aimed in her direction.

"Follow me." Soji strode cautiously into the channel created by the invisible field. "Closely."

She hopped the compressed vegetation, and slid into the wide rocky laceration made from the crash long ago. The ghosts of her past seemed to follow her, their voices reproachful in the creaking brush and flailing leaves. Good people had died to keep the matrix out of ahuu hands. Could she surrender what they'd given their lives for?

"Keep up," she growled.

She understood Iex more now than she had then, but no amount of life saving would make her truly trust him. He was too alien. They'd spent too many years hating each other. If she gave him the matrix it might destroy his world and kill his people, and she didn't hate him that much, not anymore.

"Your people are rash and unpredictable," she said suddenly as she leapt across a mat of spiked coils that oozed a blood-colored fluid, unaware she was going to speak.

"That is a truly horrifying assessment... from a human." The ahu's head bent quickly in amusement.

"It takes one to know one, huh?" Soji chuckled. Maybe they weren't so dissimilar after all.

Something slid silently through the branches overhead. It blotting out the feeble rays of the twilight sun as it passed, leaving flecks of unsettling darkness on the jungle floor. Soji glanced up. "What...."

The thing landed. It hit them like a crashing starship, an oblong ochre-colored mass of limbs and teeth as big as the shuttle. Iex tumbled. The shock of impact forced him to the ground as Soji screamed and the enormous creature bounced away from the repressor field.

The ahuu looked dazed. In the confusion, the field generator had broken free from his harness, coming to rest in a shallow depression in the dry bedrock centimeters from Soji's outstretched hand. She snatched it. Her first thought was to run, but there was nowhere to go. The shuttle would lead offworld. She didn't want that. She didn't know what she wanted.

"Hand it back."

"Go home, Iex." She danced back as the ahuu struggled to regain his footing. "You can't have the matrix, nobody can."

"What will you do? Leave me here?" He asked, moving slowly towards her. "Kill me?"

"No, that's where we differ," she said.

The object in her hand grew hot. Its orange glow faded, and the field shrank with a sighing sound as the surrounding jungle decompressed.

"It's failing. Give it to me. Now." Iex rushed forward.

Soji dived out of the way. The emitter created a small tunnel through the foliage in front of her, and she ran. Branches cracked. An alien bellow roared through the forest. She heard a hiss, and one of the long bolts from the ahuu's crossbow shattered a heart-shaped burl near her head.

"You can't escape this world, Soji."

"No," she said breathlessly into the translator. "But you should. That path from the ship won't last long. You might just make it."

He howled again, but it was further away. He couldn't hope to follow her. She knew it, and she knew he did too. She really didn't want him dead. There was no point in it. This was her task, a continuation of the mission she'd failed a decade earlier, a price to be paid for her foolishness.

As long as that matrix existed it would be a temptation, a lure to the greedy or desperate. If they came looking, more would die. If they found it intact and managed to take it off planet, then the carnage would start all over again.

She rushed on through the jungle, past once-familiar rock formations made monstrous by the intrusion of deadly flora, and onto a low mound facing the rounded opening of a cave. Flattened spike-covered vines slapped listlessly at her feet, still trying to kill her even as they died.

Bleached yellow bones protruded like new shoots all around her. The hill was made from them, the remains of the nintti. This was where they'd first used the matrix. It was also where they'd made their last stand against it.

A silver teardrop hovered directly above her, briefly peeling the jungle back before lifting away. Iex's voice squealed through her translator. "This is madness."

"Glad to see you made it."

"You, Soji, are rash and unpredictable," he said as the capsule dwindled upward.

"That is a truly horrifying assessment...." She laughed. The ahuu had a sense of humor after all.

"For a human...." was the last thing she heard before turning toward the cave mouth. It was time to take care of that matrix, one way or the other.

About the Author

D. A. D'AMICO takes his writing far too seriously. He allows his characters to walk all over him, making demands in loud voices, eating all the chips, and wrecking up the joint. If it weren't for their typing skills, he'd throw the bunch of them out. He's had nearly eighty works published in the last decade in venues such as Daily Science Fiction, and Shock Totem, and his personal favorite, MYTHIC. He's a winner of L. Ron Hubbard's prestigious Writers of the Future award, volume XXVII, as well as the 2017 Write Well award. His website is: http://www.dadamico.com. Facebook: authordadamico, and on painfully rare occasions twitter: @dadamico.

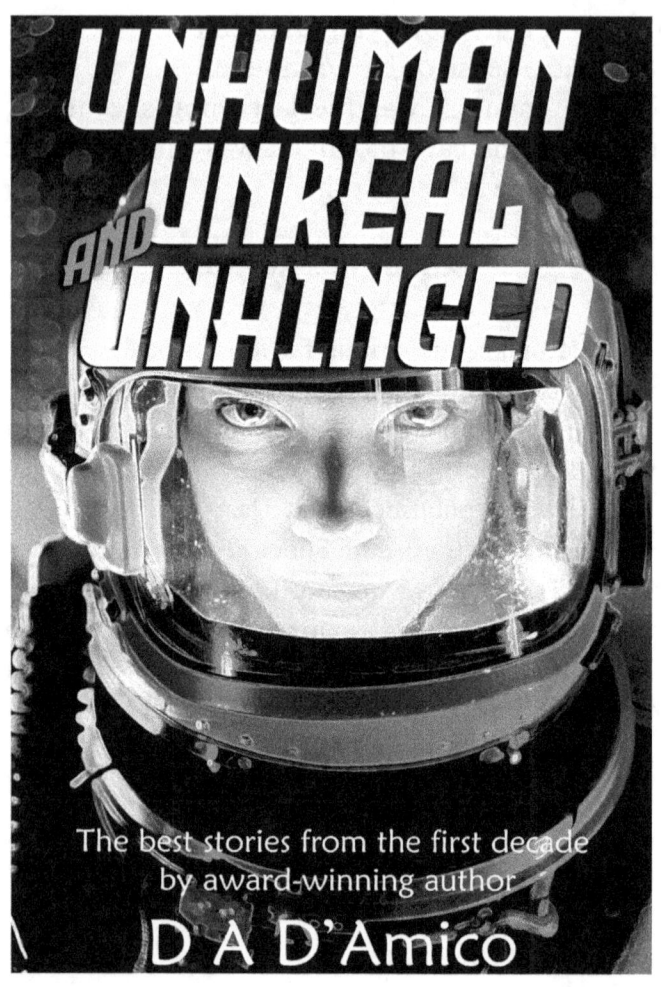

For the Land and the King Are One

By Margaret R. Taylor

IJAY CHOUDHARY GREW up in a colonial administrative district at the western edge of the British Raj. The district of Dewar had once been the Kingdom of Dewar, but the British came with rifles and gunpowder and drove King Jodha out. In school Vijay pledged fealty to Queen Victoria, the source of all life. As long as the students did so, the acacia trees would grow and the rainy season would come.

When he was nine years old, his father brought him on a business trip to Assam. The senior Choudhary needed to clear up a bookkeeping problem for a Tea Company.

When they boarded the steam train, Vijay gaped at how big and black it was, and coughed when he got downwind of the smokestack. He pressed his nose to the glass the entire trip east. British soldiers patrolled the highways with eight-legged mechanical walkers. British engineers retrofitted the villages with birds' nests of overhead electrical wires. British mining machines stripped the hillsides, leaving stairsteppy pits with pools of tailings at the bottom that glowed an eerie copper blue.

They disembarked and a mechanical carriage with a chauffeur took them to the plantation house. When the carriage engine rumbled to a stop, a man in coattails put a hand on his father's shoulder and drew him away. Vijay pushed himself out of his seat.

His sandals sank into mud, which schlupped when he pulled his feet up. The air smelled like earth and vegetation. Hills rose up on either side of him, terraced with rows of tea bushes so the land looked like corduroy—a world of green upon green upon green. He had never been outside of the desert before.

He stumbled past the road, past the plantation house, to the rows with his mouth hanging open. The tea laborers sweated in broad-brimmed hats out here. They'd strapped baskets as big as they were to their backs, and they worked down the rows of tea bushes, plucking buds and throwing them over their shoulders.

The watchman stood at attention at the end of the row, a big-bearded Assamese man wearing a turban and a brilliant red coat. He held a rifle over one shoulder.

"Why is it so green here?" Vijay said.

The watchman gave him a glance, then returned to watching over the laborers. His coat had very nice brass buttons. "Because of the queen."

Vijay knew a little about Queen Victoria, but he wanted more. He planted his feet in the mud. Adults would keep talking if he stared at them long enough. It always worked.

The watchman sighed. "You see them?" He gestured with his rifle to the laborers. "They sign five-year contracts to a Tea Company. The Tea Company signs a charter with the queen. She's strong, boy. An empire of half a billion."

One of the laborers loosened the straps of his basket and set it down.

"But how does she—"

"Run along, now." The watchman strode forward. "Hey, you there!"

Vijay wouldn't learn any more here. He kept walking.

In time he came to the edge of the Tea Company's zone of control. Stretched between fence posts, a soap-bubble film of magic hummed and swirled with colors. He put his hand in the bubble and it passed through.

His hand blurred on the other side and the magic prickled on his skin. He took his hand out. He touched the magic again, up to the elbow, then up to the shoulder. He took his hand out and looked at it. Why would a Tea Company create a magic wall that didn't do anything?

He followed along the magic fence, and twenty paces later kicked a shred of sari on the footpath. He picked it up, and another scrap hung from a tree branch, swaying like a dead animal, and... a laborer had tried to force herself through the fence. She must have been a woman. But he couldn't tell because the corpse was inside out.

When he got home, he scoured his father's shelves for all the books about charter magic he could get. He had to know how to make it stop.

LONG BEFORE THE reign of Victoria, the British Isles had a king named Bron. He murdered his uncle to claim the throne of Wessex, then he gathered loyal men, armed them with spears and armored them with leather and bronze, and rampaged the other warlords on the island. He forged east to Essex. North to Mercia. West to Dumnonia. Bron's men burned down villages. They burned charters and made the survivors swear fealty to him. Year after year, he conquered and conquered, aiming to become *bretwalda*, the wide-ruler of all England.

Then at the Battle of Ellandun, a Celt stabbed the king in the crotch.

Bron's men strung the Celt up on a pole and poured boiling oil on him, but the damage had been done. Crippled, Bron retreated to his fort. He sat by the river all day and fished. In Wessex the soil washed away with the rain. The wheat wouldn't sprout. The sheep wouldn't lamb.

This is the nature of charter magic: king, kingdom, and every living being inside it are bound to each other by invisible threads of power. A charter sets the rules of the bonds. The people swear fealty to their king, and all the hopes and dreams they invest in him make him strong. The strength of the king's body lends strength to the land and the people. If the bonds break, the land breaks.

By 1890 the British Empire wrapped around the world like a spider's web with millions of strands. Vijay's bond to the queen was simple because he was Dewari and Dewar was a useless stretch of desert. He just had to swear to serve her. But tea was valuable, and Assamese laborers filled tea crates that sailed in steamships to Britain, so laborers were valuable. The Tea Companies preferred to keep their laborers in one place. They wrote their charters to kill.

Vijay needed more books.

A T THE AGE of seventeen Vijay bought a jodhpur suit he couldn't afford. It had blue fabric with a gold jacquard weave, manufactured on punchcard looms at the heart of the British Empire. He shaved, he chewed cloves, he went to the right parties. He cornered a commissioner for education behind a rhododendron bush, smiled and bowed. In perfect English he said that in order to perfect the Raj's loyalty to the empire, he wished to join the bureaucracy. He would become a colonial charter magician—the ambition of a model coolie.

Surely the commissioner would hear his heart pounding in his ears, his lie. He had to alter charter magic so colonials could live without Queen Victoria. To do that, he needed all the books in Kings College London.

The National Indian Association awarded him a university scholarship.

When he disembarked from the steamship, he gasped from the cold. He ran a hand along the back of his neck and it came away wet—London fog had condensed on his collar. Edifices of stone and brass stretched over him, three, four, five stories high. The city roared with the sound of machinery. He took a deep breath and stepped down the gangplank.

He rented a room above a steam-powered tuba workshop. The landlady brought him up plates of bread with mushy peas. He went to bed huddled under everything he owned as the clicking of the radiator kept him awake until dawn.

By day, the sun never shone. Everything he touched, his fingers pulled up a fine layer of soot. And these British, they wouldn't look at him, their eyes slid off this brown-skinned young man. The loneliness was miserable. But his charter bond ... he felt healthy enough. In his room he would prod himself and take his pulse. If he was this close to the queen, the source of all life, should he feel different?

He slid between classes at the university, keeping his eyes on the floor tiles. Other colonials brushed past him in the throng of British: Egyptians with their long white caftans, Canadians with their flattened vowels, Indians. He didn't speak to them. But once in the chemistry building, a young man handed him a pamphlet by the Indian Independence Movement. It said that the colonial districts of the Raj could find their royal bloodlines from before the British came. The people could transfer their fealty to the old kings and write new charters. Independent ones.

Horror ran through Vijay as he read the words. He took the pamphlet to an incinerator and dropped it in. If he associated with these independence people, he would get caught. Nobody must know his crazier idea: maybe people didn't have to have a monarch at all.

I N HIS ROOM, wrapped in a blanket, Vijay cracked open a book for a class project. Elective monarchy.

In cold climates such as Iceland and some parts of Siberia, the people could make it work. On midwinter's night, all the free men would gather in their longhouses to elect a new king. But the elected king was not of royal blood, so his body couldn't hold up to the strain of keeping a kingdom alive. The farmers would raise their reindeer or their rye and the king would wither. By fall the king would be bedridden.

Every winter, these men must destroy their charter and write a new one, and let the old king die. If they didn't, they faced winter eternal. One place that used to call itself Norway had become a blasted mountain range of bare rock because the air was too cold for snow to fall. Explorers reported that the sun dimmed the moment they crossed the border from the Kingdom of Sweden. The survivors escaped with frostbite and shattered equipment.

Elective monarchy was close, so close to the government he wanted. But too unstable.

A FEW WEEKS later he searched the library's Royal Society journals for monographs on Norway when he rounded a corner. A woman sat at a study table, deep in a book. An Indian woman. She closed the book and he glimpsed the title: *Fundamenta autem Necromantia.*

He froze. He shouldn't get too close to people. But she knew necromancy, and he had suspicions about the government of Hell. And … he hadn't said a word to another colonial in six months.

The woman raised her eyebrows.

Impulse propelled him forward, and he sat at the table. "Is that any good?"

She tilted the book open to show him text in Latin. He couldn't understand a word. "It's dense reading."

A Dewari accent. Images burst in on him of sun through acacia trees, the cardamom sweets he used to have as a boy. "My name's Vijay."

"Raka," she said. "Odd of you to take an interest in necromancy."

"I'm a curious person." She wouldn't believe that half-truth for one moment. His hands sweated. "So what do demons do?"

He studied at that section of the library more and more.

On days off they walked London streets, racing ahead of Raka's chaperone, dodging mechanical carriages. They got rained on. They searched for anywhere that served vegetarian food and made a game out of who could discover the most disgusting English dish. Pickled eggs! Bubble and squeak! Crumpets!

Their conversations circled a blank space. Raka had a reason to study necromancy in the heart of London, but she wasn't telling. Vijay had a plan, too. He couldn't tell her, not yet.

Meanwhile, he kept an ear on the Independence Movement people. Dewar had a problem. Stealthy men had combed the orphanages for the old king's heir. They'd given every farm boy in the district a look over for identifying marks and sent rangers into the grasslands to see if any she-tiger had taken in an abandoned baby. Nothing. No heir to the throne.

Then surely he was right, they should abolish kings. Dewar had no other option.

One night he and Raka hauled their books to the Dean's Hall, the only place on campus with a fireplace. Raka balanced a book on her knee in an armchair. Vijay sat at her feet with his legs tucked under him. The chaperone had fallen asleep.

He shifted his weight. Was the old woman really asleep? Could anybody out in the hall hear them?

He put a hand on her hand. "Is Hell a republic?"

"Yes." The firelight made her black eyes shine a deep amber. The intensity of her regard made him quail to his core.

She must know. The insane plot he had nursed for ten years.
"The demons pay for it," she said. "They have rivers of molten lead and lakes of fire. Sulfurous fumes that rise from the ground. Clouds of darkness visible."
"But they can do it?"
"Vijay." She squeezed his hand. "They keep me talking. They ask for tea and a chat so they can stay in their chalk circle a little longer. They're proud creatures. So proud. But their republic wears them out."

V IJAY RETURNED TO the Raj and got a job with the colonial bureaucracy. The Raj stationed him in the Thar Desert, where he consulted with engineers on hydrological projects. He counted the queen's subjects and calculated who needed to move where to make the water flow. The year 1910 came and went and Victoria hadn't aged for thirty years. Some people whispered. What would happen? No queen had ruled half a billion subjects before. Vijay kept his head close to his desk and collected data from the agency archives.

The Iroquois Confederacy had devised a system of power sharing. The clan mothers from each of the five nations chose representatives to meet and make decisions. The mothers and the representatives were nobility of a sort, and the people spread their fealty over dozens of nobles, so they didn't wear out. The system worked for a while. But when the American colonists rebelled in the 1700's, the Iroquois declared for the rebels. The war ended in disaster.

Good to know. A people needed more than a strong charter to maintain independence from Britain. They needed men, guns, and money.

Meanwhile, the Indian Independence Movement organized sit-down strikes, boycotts, and raids to blow up British gunpowder stocks. They searched libraries, genealogies, and census records, found the old royal lines and planned the fealty transfer. Vijay struggled as he read the news. What a half measure, to switch one monarch for another. But it was time for him to offer help. He wrote them a letter.

THEN, TOO SOON, the governor-general declared independence.

Vijay had picked his kettle up when the windows rattled, his stomach dropped and he grabbed onto the counter for support. He felt like he'd ridden one of those British lifts when the cable snapped and he plummeted to his death. Death was too close to the truth. The governor-general had just severed the colonial Raj's bonds of fealty to Queen Victoria.

The dresser with the gas burner, the nightstand, the mattress on the floor, the books in stacks on the floor, all still there. He felt the same. Unbelievable. He was no longer attached to a queen. One would think he would fall over and die, but he of all people knew that death by queen deprivation took a while.

He switched the burner off before he smothered the room. His mug had shattered at his feet, and tea seeped into the floorboards—turmeric tea. He had lost his taste for Assam years ago. He mopped up with a rag, then ran his fingers along the floor, feeling for tiny shards of ceramic.

He'd expected this. The Independence Movement had worked furiously, writing new charters, ready for their severance from Victoria. The longer they took, the more likely she discovered the treachery. They could not wait any longer. So they'd declared independence, leaving half the colonial districts without a monarch. Like Dewar.

They had a plan. While the Independence people fought their war, Dewar would call in a team of colonial charter magicians to find a solution. Like Vijay. A *national* charter magician, if he survived.

He threw a change of clothes into a steamer case and then

magic books: histories of charter magic through the ages, analyses of harmonic balance between king and people, treatises on agriculture and medicine. Maybe if he kept himself busy with these normal tasks, his heart wouldn't pound so hard.

He checked his hand as he lifted a book. Steady, so far.

He hauled his cases down the boardinghouse stairs. Thar desert heat shimmered over flat pink roofs. The leaves of the acacia trees hung dead still. A dog barked. The air tasted metallic, or maybe that was his imagination.

He stacked his cases at the side of the road, bounced on his feet. Now was no time to panic. He knew what he needed to do. But how?

A man in provisional government dun rode up. Vijay studied the man's face. He looked like all the blood had run out of him. So he'd felt the drop, too.

Yesterday, messengers such as him had all worn red coats with gold braid, as befitted the British Crown. At the last moment the Independence Movement had calculated they could, the bureaucrats would have swapped their uniforms, red for dun, and transferred their fealty to the new government. Turncoats.

The messenger fumbled at the case on his saddle and pulled out a paper. Vijay snatched it out of his hands.

Dewar had summoned him home.

WHEN HE ARRIVED in the capital, the dirt roads and acacia trees seemed how he remembered them as a boy, yet trucks full of sandbags and rations competed with mules to cross the street and soldiers bustled everywhere. It was getting hot. The provisional government put him up in a building that was once a regional branch of the agriculture ministry, now converted for the war effort.

He set his cases in the doorway of his assigned office,

a room of peach-tan limestone to keep out the heat, with a window that overlooked the street. An iron desk held some other bureaucrat's things. If he was honest with himself, the stair climb had made him wheeze. He felt off.

All right. He stacked the other man's papers in alphabetical order and put them in a drawer. He cleared off the desk hutch, unpacked magic books, and unfolded a camp bed. How long would he live here, until he'd completed his impossible task? Dewar must survive without a king. The spies had failed—still no sign of the heir to the throne.

He was setting an abacus on the desk when he heard movement in the hall. A curly-haired man in a green jodhpur suit came carrying a valise. He looked well.

The man placed his hands together and bowed. "I am Nagendra from the Kingdom of Peshwa. A charter magician like you. I'm here to help."

That explained his health. The neighboring colonial district, Peshwa, had installed its new king last week. Their new *prince*, but clearly their prince was good enough for them.

In the old days, the kingdoms of Dewar and Peshwa had fought many wars.

Vijay put his hands together. "I'm from around here. It's good to be back."

For a few moments, Vijay straightened magic books that didn't need straightening. Nagendra came into the office and peered out the window. The distinct metallic taste in the air couldn't be good for the Peshwan's lungs, charter bond or not. At least Vijay had that.

"Your initial thoughts?" said Nagendra.

He'd given the matter two decades of thought, but he still didn't have an answer, only half-solutions. He'd never get a republic to work. "Yes. We find as many nobles as possible and we spread the charter out on them."

"The simplest thing would be for Dewar to merge with

Peshwa. We should resolve this quickly so we have strong men for the war."

Vijay pressed his lips together, nodded, and let the man leave. Nagendra only recommended something that benefited his own kingdom, it was understandable. Vijay was the crazy one, cooking an anti-monarchist plot.

D AWN CAME WITH hot, still air. The thorn scrubs that crowded around the town pump turned brown at the edges. A bowl of millet rolls sat on Vijay's blotter; he'd taken a couple of bites and abandoned them because he couldn't keep them down. He rubbed his eyes.

From two decades of research into charter magic, he had derived general rules. The king had to come from royal blood. The common people had to swear fealty to him. He had to stay healthy.

And if weak kings made harsh climates, the relationship worked the other way as well. In islands in the Pacific, tundras, and deserts, the people could bend the rules. They got away with chieftains or nobles. Kings who ruled for set numbers of years. Ruling councils.

Dewar was a desert, so they had some hope.

Suppose … one dredged up every Dewari with a drop of aristocratic blood. They already had, searching for the heir to the throne. The nobles could form a sort of parliament and elect one of their own as the new king. Would that work?

How his head ached. The thing was, they didn't need another parliament. The provisional government worked fine coordinating the war effort and writing the laws. They only needed a king at all so they could breathe.

He reached for another book.

W ITH INDEPENDENCE, THE colonial Raj became a collection of kingdoms only allied because of their war with Britain. In Sri Lanka men dragged the scion of the snake-gods out of the jungle and planted him on the throne. In Assam thirty percent of the people died instantly; the survivors rioted, reorganized into workers' co-ops, and swore a conditional fealty to the king of Bhutan. Vijay wished them luck. Rice and sorghum wilted. A typhoon struck Bombay out of season. Disorder reigned in the port cities as white people and high-castes who could pay crowded the ships, getting out.

Rumors came to them. The people of London reported an eldritch screech that rattled windows and bones. Queen Victoria made no public appearances. Losing two hundred and fifty million subjects at once had not been good for her.

The British sent gunships to Madras, Calcutta, and Bangalore. Meanwhile, Rhodesians attacked British outposts and even colonists as far away as Boston threw a shipment of tea overboard.

Raka commanded demons at Fort Jaisalmer. Well, she summoned them, explained the situation, and scuffed the chalk circle. A crew of blue-skinned, many-armed, animal-headed creatures loped, rolled, and slithered into the desert and battled the eight-legged walkers the British sent. The machines threw quicklime and burning pitch as the demons sabered their legs out from under them.

AFTERNOON HEAT SHIMMERED on the dirt outside. The thorn scrubs had shriveled and curled. Vijay felt a knot in his guts. When was the last time he had slept? But he had it, an ugly solution.

It was *ugly*. A mishmash of the Iroquois and Norwegian solutions, with shades of Polynesian chieftain rule. It might work. He still had to convince the provisional government to choose it over merger with Peshwa.

They wouldn't. Of course Dewar would swallow its pride and choose security with a foreign king. It wasn't personal.

They needed strength *now* so they could win a war. Decades of work, and he'd only derived a mediocre way to live without a king. He had never figured out how to break the rules of charter magic.

He put the papers down and with difficulty descended the stairs to the temporary mail station. Everything was temporary right now. He fished his mail out of the cubby.

Raka had written him a letter from the front. When the demons didn't need her, she ran behind the supply lines, evacuating villages before the mechanical walkers came. At a field hospital, she'd found an orphan with a birthmark the shape of an antelope between his shoulder blades. The magical animal of Dewar. The chinkara.

She had found the heir to the throne of Dewar.

The despair made him want to laugh. Laughter sent a stab of pain through his ribs and he clutched the table for support. Dewar didn't have to become a client state to Peshwa. He could end the ache in his guts and the poison in the air right now, just by showing this letter to an officer in the provisional government. He could save his district by giving up on all the work he'd ever done.

His hands tightened on the letter. Raka had written to him, not to the provisional government.

He knew what he had to do. He had to burn this letter.

H E REWROTE HIS proposal from scratch. Dewar knew it had an ancient and proud lineage somewhere. The idea of a king, and fealty to that idea, mattered more than the king himself. All right, the men of Norway ran into trouble without a royal body in charge, but look: they knew their king was common. So they didn't believe in him hard enough. So the magic broke, so the man died. Dewar knew their king was royal … somewhere, so they could do better.

The Dewari should teach old books at the village schools. They should memorize the known names of their lineage. Jaswant I, the founder, who spontaneously generated out of desert sand. Bhagwant I, who defeated the Peshwans with an army of antelopes. Bhagwant II, who begat Shekha, who begat Jodha, who is lost.

The people should sweep the dust out of the royal palace and scrub the walls down, hang curtains, string up lights, and burn incense. Everyone who could manage the journey should hold a feast in the great hall, with a space at the head of the table to await the return of their king. Someday. They should arrange the feast straight away, then repeat once every year at Diwali. With a few tweaks to the charter, Dewar could look the world in the eye and call itself a kingdom.

Lies. So were the lines of charter code that he attached that would make the rituals work. All lies. A scholar should devote his life to the pursuit of truth and here he was tricking Dewar to swear fealty to a baby in a village hospital. But better to betray truth than his other plan, his crazy plan to come as close to a republic as he could in this world.

He pulled his papers together and submitted them to the governor of the Dewari colonial district.

THE GOVERNOR APPROVED Vijay's plan. So the Peshwan didn't get his way—Vijay got some pleasure out of that.

The evening of the feast, he sat in his office that didn't belong to him, not writing, chewing his pen, looking out the window. In all his research, he had never seen a people separate their king from their government. Maybe the charter would fail. Maybe he had doomed them all.

As the sun touched the horizon his chest loosened and his pulse grew stronger. He put his hands on the desk and drew his first full breath in weeks. It had worked. The pigeon peas would come with the rainy season.

THAT NIGHT, IN the dark office, Vijay knelt at his steamer case. Down the hall, the Peshwan snored. Vijay took a moment to relish breathing. Deep and effortless. A cool breeze lifted his hair and an exultation of stars spread across the sky. His district—his *country*, Dewar. There was a faraway boom and rumble, and the breeze carried the scent of cordite.

He set the last books in and snapped the case shut. The rest of his things lay by the door, a dark pile like a hungry ghost come to get him.

Two hours until dawn. Plenty of time to get out of here. The provisional government would consider him a deserter, and he would let them, considering what he had just done to Dewar. He would return to his boardinghouse long enough to destroy documents and make himself disappear. Then he would ride to Fort Jaisalmer. He would find the boy at the hospital and prepare a good home for him … rice merchants would do. He would apply for a job as the boy's tutor.

He would teach the boy charter magic and the history of the world. Kings were normal people when they took the throne. But power over life and death twisted minds, and power led to beheadings and boiling oil and pogroms and charter designs that turned laborers inside out. The wheel of history churned over and over, crushing common people in the dust.

Maybe this time in Dewar, the people would swear fealty to their king. The king would live, the charter bonds would remain intact. The government would run the country like a republic. The king would pursue a career in the civil service, and marry and have children, Vijay would see to that. Maybe, *maybe,* the king would come out right in the head this time.

He hefted his case with new strength because of the thread that connected him to a faraway baby.

Raka had a war to win. Him? He would make sure the boy loved his country the way it was, bowing to an empty throne.

About the Author

MARGARET R. TAYLOR lives in Twin Cities with a computer programmer and a retired street cat. A botanist by training, she brings her love of science to the magic systems in her fiction. She can be found planting milkweeds in the garden and making home pickles. Check out her blog at www.steamtrainsandghosts.com.

Many stories have been written already about the approaching end of industrial civilization: about the great tragedies and the small triumphs, about struggles spread out across landscapes and struggles just as bitter within individual hearts, about the people who survive and the ones who don't. One theme that's been unfairly neglected in deindustrial fiction is love. As iconic SF author Theodore Sturgeon noted, the little things go on—and among those little things are human relationships, blossoming in the most unlikely settings. This anthology includes ten stories and three poems about love in the deindustrial future, by turns ethereal and earthy, traumatic and tender—but all of them ending with a promise of happily ever after...

"In times of such huge confusion, the little things go on. During the 'Ten Days that Shook the World' the cafés and theaters of Moscow and Petrograd stayed open, people fell in love, sued each other, died, shed sweat and tears; and some of the tears were tears of laughter." ~ Theodore Sturgeon, "The Hurkle is a Happy Beast"

Available in print and eBook editions!

The *Inter States* Series:

What if America failed to deci-sively turn away from fossil-fuel dependence when it still had the capital and geopolitical security to do so?

What if the disappearance of America's middle class became a permanent condition, and, along with it, the disappearance of na-tional popular democracy in all by name only?

What if the effects of climate change started to significantly affect U.S. politics and economics?

"Crisp, fast-paced, and un-comfortably plausible....a new series set in a crumbling, dysfunctional United States in the not too distant future. Readers who want something more interesting and chal-lenging than one more help-ing of yesterday's futures will find Meima's narrative well worth their time."

-John Michael Greer

Teacher for the Apple

By Sarina Dorie

DORIS FAIRVIEW SQUINTED at the second-grade class list through her bifocals. "Chris Hernandez?"

A six-year-old fidgeting with his overall straps raised his hand. "Here! I'm here, Mrs. Fairview!" He practically jumped up and down with excitement it being their day.

Doris smiled. This was why she adored second-graders. They loved school and their teachers and life. She'd first become a teacher because she enjoyed drawing out that spark of wonder and awe from eager learners. There was no greater feeling than making the impossible possible. She moved on down the list. "Rainbow Jackson?"

A little girl raised her hand.

Doris checked her off. "Erik Jensen?"

A blond boy with brown eyes raised his hand. Doris took off her glasses, squinted and then put them back on. He looked so much like her best friend in second grade. His name also had been Erik, and he too had worn an argyle sweater vest despite the September heat. The little boy smiled, revealing a missing front tooth. A sense of deja vu swept over Doris. It was a coincidence, she told herself. She'd taught other Eriks who were blond, and they hadn't reminded her of her friend from so long ago.

Doris moved on to the next child. Still, she couldn't help sneaking glances at Erik Jensen. Later while students were writing or drawing about their summer vacation at their desks, she studied his chubby cheeks and familiar dimples. She'd taught a student named Erik a few years back who had the same fair, wavy hair. He'd filled his notebook with scratchy hieroglyphic-like lines during recess and used advanced words like "peers" and "acquaintance."

Erik looked up. Doris smiled. He returned her smile and went back to writing about summer vacation. Unlike some of the other second graders, he could write a complete sentence. Doris strolled past to the next row of students.

Kayla Pierson picked her nose and wiped it on one of the desks. Doris stepped forward and handed the second-grader a tissue. "Honey, use this."

Kayla sniffled and kept writing. "No, it's okay. I don't need it."

Doris crouched so that she was eye level with the girl. "Yes, you do, Kayla. You need to be sanitary so you don't pass on germs to others." Doris was about to bestow her hygiene mantra on the child, "Share everything—except your germs," but two children kicking each other caught her attention, and she rushed away to separate them.

This was what happened when they gave her a class of thirty-four six-year-olds and no educational assistants. Ten years ago she would have had an educational assistant and taught twenty children at the most. These days she barely managed to babysit this many. So much had changed in her forty-six years of teaching.

She separated the two fighting children, already feeling worn out even though it wasn't ten o'clock yet. She hoped she hadn't forgotten to take her heart medication. Doris was still worrying about this when she heard Erik say to Kayla, "Share everything—except your germs."

Doris's spine went rigid. This was their first day; how could he possibly have known her mantra? She glanced over her shoulder at Erik. He leaned toward Kayla and whispered something while pointing at the tissue box.

Over the next several days, Doris noticed how easily Erik picked up on her routine, how impeccable his math was despite his youth, and how he brought his notebook out to recess and jotted down notes in it between games. While he played on the jungle gym with the other children, Doris slipped from her shady post under the oak tree and headed toward the spot he'd left it. Her feet crunched over dried leaves that only days ago had been golden and lush. She picked up the notebook.

Written in vertical columns were lines that resembled hieroglyphics. Her heart sped up. Surely it wasn't possible. Now that she got a better look, she realized it wasn't hieroglyphics; it was similar to a runic alphabet like they had used long ago in Scandinavia. If she took the book back to her desk, she could use the Internet to see if it said anything. Her friend, Erik from long ago, had been Scandinavian and had told her stories about Vikings, gods and immortals. Her favorite stories had been about the Valkyries, beautiful maidens who selected the best of the slain warriors to go to Valhalla.

She closed the book. Erik stood in front of her, out of breath and flushed in the cheeks. She gasped in surprise and stepped back. Her heel slipped on a clump of slimy leaves. She would have tumbled back, but Erik caught her arm.

He was unusually strong for a child.

"Are you all right, Mrs. Fairview?"

She cleared her throat. "Yes, excuse me."

"May I have my book back?" He held out his hand.

She did her best to feign surprise. "Oh? Is this yours?" She handed it to him.

One eyebrow lifted, giving the six-year-old an expression of maturity that was unnatural on such a young face.

"Tell me about the writing in your book. Is it another language?" she asked.

He kicked at a pile of bark chips. "It isn't writing. It's nothing. Just my scribbles."

Doris lifted an eyebrow of her own. "It looks like you take breaks from playing to take notes on the other children."

His eyes narrowed as he looked into hers. "Looks can be deceiving, Mrs. Fairview."

D ORIS SCOOTED AROUND pairs of second graders reading with fifth graders in the school library. Little Lydia sat next to an older girl on the beanbag chair reading a Barbie story. Marco sat next to a girl with braces reading about Spider-Man.

Doris meandered around the reading children, checking off names on her list. She opened the book she'd tucked under her arm, a yearbook from fifteen years ago. She perused the pictures, looking for a child she'd taught named Erik at Centennial Elementary. She found a black and white photo of a boy named Erik Lundren. He had the same chubby cheeks and dimples. Only, he wasn't in her class that year. He was in Cheryl Woodlawn's class. She could have sworn she'd had an Erik about fifteen years ago. Maybe he'd been held back, and she'd had him the year after? They used to do that in the old days if kids missed too many lessons or didn't get the main concepts, though too many parents protested it hurt their children's self-esteem. Now kids always passed the second grade—even when they failed.

Doris returned the yearbook and selected the following year. He wasn't in that one. She found an Erik she'd taught in a yearbook from twelve years before, though he'd been absent on picture day, so she couldn't confirm her suspicion.

Erik sat with impeccable posture next to a fifth grader sprawled across a carpet made to look like train tracks. Doris meandered toward them, curious to see what Erik had selected. Probably another Norse legend. He often picked those. Only yesterday he'd been telling her about a Scandinavian fable with the gods of Asgard guarding golden apples and before that it was another tale of the Valkyries.

Erik's fifth grade partner, Ivan, read slowly, enunciating each word. "'Someone gently raping, raping—'"

Doris' mortification subsided when Erik coughed and corrected the older boy. "The word is rapping. Two p's make a soft 'a' sound."

"Oh. 'Someone gently rapping, rapping at my chamber door. 'Tis some visitor,' I muttered, 'tapping at my chamber door—Only this and nothing more.' That doesn't even make sense. Is he, like what, dancing and singing?"

"Rapping means knocking," Erik said. Doris hadn't even realized there was any Edgar Allen Poe in the school library. Then again, her students rarely ventured beyond the picture book section. Had the older child brought this book from the other end of the library?

The fifth grader cupped his hands around his mouth and became a human beatbox. He rapped out the text he'd been reading. Other students in the library giggled. Doris put a finger to her lips and shook her head.

Erik tore the book away from his partner and read, "'Ah, distinctly I remember it was in the bleak December; and each separate dying ember wrought its ghost upon the floor.'" He looked over his shoulder, his eyes locking on Doris's.

A chill coursed through her.

M E! ME! I want to go next!" shouted students. They sat in a circle on the worn gray carpet in her classroom.

Doris sat in a chair in the circle, keeping order as they all raised their hands to be the next to share during show-and-tell. Her entire body felt weary, and it wasn't even noon yet. She was old, too old to be teaching a class this big, but she couldn't afford retirement yet.

"Mrs. Fairview only picks quiet children," Erik said over the chaos. "Look how Juan is sitting quietly raising his hand. Maybe she'll pick him."

The students quieted. Doris sighed in relief. She picked Juan next. He spoke about his teddy bear. It didn't escape her eye that Erik jotted down notes in his book in his Runic code. It came as no surprise Erik chose to share something of his Norse heritage. He held up a pendant with a Celtic looking tree. "This represents the location where Asgard is located. When the Valkyries bring fallen warriors there, some are chosen to go to Odin's hall, Valhalla. They drink lots of mead, fight battles and party. Some go to Freyja's hall, Folkvangr. The afterlife is a little more relaxed there." An impish smile played across his lips. "Do you like to drink mead, Mrs. Fairview?"

"What's mead?" Kayla asked.

Doris eyed Erik warily. "No, I prefer tea."

After show-and-tell, Erik followed her to her desk. "Mrs. Fairview, you're looking tired today. Let me be your special helper so these children don't wear you out."

She laughed uneasily. He didn't sound at all like a normal child. She didn't know what to make of him. He passed out boxes of crayons for her and instructed students in the day's art lesson, using the same vocabulary she would have.

Afterward he went back to his desk and jotted down another note. He stared at her with rapt attention. Every time she spoke, whether during studies or recess, he wrote in Runic in his book. It unnerved her for a child to pay such close attention to anything at school. It was unnatural.

He might not ever have been taking notes on the other students, but on her all along.

I BROUGHT YOU a present." Erik set a shiny, golden apple on Doris's desk next to the wilting flowers she didn't have the heart to throw away yet. She stared at the apple over her bifocals, wondering what kind of temptation this was. It smelled like autumn and sweet childhood memories.

Sunlight danced over the yellow skin, making it glow amongst the stacks of papers and school supplies on her cluttered desk.

Erik smiled up at her. "Mrs. Fairview, you look especially pretty today. Is it a special occasion?"

She smoothed her wrinkled hands over her flower-printed dress. "Thank you. Aren't you sweet? Yes, it's parent-teacher conferences this afternoon. I noticed your parents didn't make an appointment with the school."

Erik smiled and shrugged.

"I wish I could meet your parents and tell them what a smart child you are." Doris opened a file on her desk and handed him a contact form. "Could you have your guardians fill this out? I tried calling to set up a conference, but the number no longer works."

Erik took the form and tucked it into his backpack.

"Can I ask . . . is your father's name also Erik?" Doris asked. "Or maybe a cousin? Older brother? You remind me of someone. . . ."

He frowned and his eyes grew distant. "We've had this conversation before, Doris."

She crossed her arms. He was getting awfully familiar. Most students didn't even know her first name.

"When? I don't remember asking you this before." Although, when she thought about it, it hadn't previously occurred to her why this Erik reminded her of the second one, but not the other blond Eriks with brown eyes who liked Norse mythology in previous years. Unless they had reminded her of him, but she couldn't recollect this detail. "*Why* don't I remember asking you about this before?"

His smile grew mischievous. "Mrs. Fairview, has anyone told you that you ask a lot of questions? Now it's only a matter of asking the right question."

D ORIS STARED AT the yellow apple on her desk. A week had passed, and it looked just as fresh and new as when Erik had first brought it to her. In that week, Erik hadn't brought back an updated form. It didn't surprise her. The child sat at his desk copying his spelling words. He glanced up and smiled a little too sweetly. He looked the picture of innocence, but she knew he was up to something.

She shook her head. Her imagination had to be getting the best of her. Maybe it was time she retired. She was old and these long days wore on her. More than that, the long evenings alone felt even longer. But if she retired, she wasn't sure what else she'd do. She'd devoted so much time and energy to her career over the years, she had alienated herself from friends and family. Instead of going out with other teachers on Friday nights, she cut out foam shapes for the following week's craft projects, researched the newest techniques for helping children with learning disabilities or planned lessons.

Now she was old and alone. The administration didn't thank her for all the extra time she put in, and the parents complained she didn't do enough to make sure their children passed. No one really appreciated what she did. Why she had done this to herself? How she would have liked to sit down in front of a toasty fire with a hot cup of tea and read a book.

"Mrs. Fairview, Ricky stole my pencil!" a little girl howled in the back.

"Have you tried problem solving?" she asked.

She drummed her fingers on the stack of yearbooks before opening the top one at her desk. Rosa Parks Elementary, 1978, Second grade, Miss Tammy Mesker's class—Erik Fullerton not pictured. Rosa Parks Elementary, 1982, Second grade, Mrs. Doris Fairview—Erik Gustafsson not pictured. In her 1998 Franklin Elementary yearbook, there were two Eriks. Erik Bjornguard was a dead ringer for her current Erik. All her Eriks had Scandinavian last names.

"Mrs. Fairview, I need to go number two!" a boy in the back called out.

She frowned at the second-grader holding the back of his pants with his hands as he jumped up and down. She hurried over as fast as her arthritic frame would allow and unsnapped his overalls. When she returned to her desk, Erik stood at the pencil sharpener. He leaned over her desk and turned the page in the 1995 Centennial year book. He studied the photograph of Erik Storstrand.

Doris sat down in her chair. Kayla was picking her nose and eating it again. Doris fought the urge to get up and correct the child. For once she had a more important matter.

She folded her hands in her lap. "Erik, do you have a question?"

Erik blew the sawdust off his sharpened pencil. "You know, Mrs. Fairview, you're my favorite teacher."

She attempted a neutral expression. "Is that so?"

"Yes, I've had a lot of teachers. Not all are as good as you are. Nor are all of them as patient and kind as you. Even when little kids are annoying or bad, you always try your best to show them how to be good." He glanced over at Kayla eating her boogers. "I wish you could live forever and keep doing what you love."

What she loved? This wasn't what she loved. She loved crossword puzzles, quiet mornings she could sleep in, and with ever-increasing yearning, snow days. Doris leaned back in her chair, trying to figure out if he was being earnest or trying to distract her.

"Why would you think I want to be a teacher forever? I'm a veteran teacher who's been working for forty-six years."

"Quite true. Working in the trenches as teachers say.

Maybe it's time for a break." The intensity of his eyes startled her. "A long deserved vacation."

"How many second grade teachers have you had?" she asked.

He giggled and shook his head.

"No, really." She pointed a finger at him. "I'm on to you."

"Do you know why I like you, Mrs. Fairview? Because you're smarter than most teachers. You teach kids to be warriors of intellect with critical thinking questions, and try to help us be better people." His expression turned sorrowful. "It would be a tragedy if something bad happened to you."

A MONTH PASSED. Every day Doris felt wearier than the last. It became increasingly difficult to remember the kids' names.

The apple on Doris's desk remained as fresh and new just as the first day Erik had given it to her. Its sweet-tart scent made her mouth water. On the day Doris gave her lunch to Enrique Kim because the boy's parents had "forgotten" to pack his again, and gotten mad the last time she'd given him the school hot lunch which they still hadn't paid for, she considered eating the apple. Then she thought about Erik, a child she would have sworn she'd taught at least four times in her career if the yearbook was any indication of proof. Instead, she walked down to vending machine in the teacher lounge on her break, becoming winded along the way. She bought a protein bar, so she could take her heart medication with something in her stomach.

When her belly grumbled as she crouched down to help Lydia with her math problems, Erik said, "Are you hungry, Mrs. Fairview? There's an apple on your desk." His expression was a little too eager. She knew that look from countless second-graders trying to play a trick on her.

She tapped an arthritic finger on a desk. "What did you do to it?"

For the first time she remembered, the little boy scowled. Not that Doris trusted her memory anymore.

The timer she'd set for recess went off. Students leapt up and ran out in a rowdy group. Doris inhaled the sweet perfume of the apple one more time before stuffing it in her desk drawer where she wouldn't see it. Its absence didn't go without notice. When Erik came back in, he grinned at her.

His eyes flashed with eagerness. "How do you feel?"

"Fine, thank you," she said.

An *ordinary* child might have come up with an *ordinary* trick like putting dog poop on an apple. She'd never suspected a second-grader of poisoning her, but she was no longer convinced this boy was a normal child. Had she asked one too many questions? Was she too close to finding out his secret?

After she had helped load the children on their buses, Doris looked up Erik's address.

His home was listed as being at 123 South A Street. Doris knew where A Street was. She passed it every day on her way home. Instead of going straight to her apartment, she turned onto A street until she approached the buildings with lower numbers. It was an industrial area of warehouses and auto shops. She didn't expect to find a building with the number 123 on it, but she did.

Doris pulled into the parking lot of a boarded-up storefront. The wind greeted her with a wintery chill as she exited her car. Her tennis shoes crunched over the gravel in the lot, and she made her way around to the door on the side of the building. Graffiti marred the concrete wall. A mangy cat backed behind a dumpster between 123 and the upholstery retailer next door.

Doris rapped at the door, and a metallic echo rang in the

air. The door creaked open. Doris poked her head inside. Her voice trembled. "Hello?"

Sunlight shone in from the highest windows on the back wall, lighting half of the immense space. Her eyes adjusted to the dimness, but she could only see so far. She removed her glasses and replaced them.

Something moved in the shadows. Her breath caught in her throat. She stepped outside and closed the door. Her heart beat wildly in her chest. What was she thinking? She was an old woman who should have retired years before, not Sherlock Holmes.

"It's just me, Mrs. Fairview," a small voice said from inside.

She opened the door again and stepped through, one hand on the door. She'd seen horror movies where doors slammed and locked on people investigating haunted houses. Well, she hadn't actually seen those movies, but she'd seen previews. She wasn't going to suffer the same fate. Her hand shook on the rusted frame.

Erik stood in his sweater vest in the middle of the warehouse. His hands were stuffed into the large pocket in the front.

"What are you doing here?" she asked, doing her best to keep her teacher tone intact. Her head swam and a wave of dizziness stole over her. She planted her feet firmly on the ground. She would not panic. She was the teacher. She was the one in charge.

"I could ask you the same," he said.

It was hard to breathe and harder still to swallow. "Do you live here by yourself? Isn't it cold? Where are your parents?"

He strolled forward. "I don't have parents."

Her voice became an octave higher. "What are you?"

He smiled. "You tell me."

"You can't be a vampire. You go out in daylight and like the cafeteria spaghetti and garlic hot lunch."

He laughed. "And I don't eat my classmates."

She tried to laugh but it brought on a sharp pain in her chest. She had to be having a muscle spasm. Or a heart attack.

"So what am I?" he asked.

"This warehouse is big enough for a spaceship. I suppose you could be . . . an alien." She struggled to form words, but her head felt foggy and her tongue fuzzy.

"That's one idea."

She unwound her scarf, feeling hot. "Yes, but that wouldn't explain the apple." She couldn't swallow the lump in her throat. Her breath came in short pants.

His eyes lit up. "You're on the right track. Did you like my apple? We're very selective about who we give apples to. You've been on my list for a long time."

Her heart beat so hard in her chest it felt like it would explode.

He stepped closer. His giddy expression turned serious. "Doris, are you all right?"

She waved him off. "The apple," she said. She could see it, but her brain was too fuzzy to think. "F-f-forbidden fruit?" If that was the case, she was safe because she hadn't eaten it.

"In some legends apples represent knowledge. Eve gave up innocence and immortality for knowledge. But in Norse mythology apples represent immortality." He toed the ground. "For those who have done something worthy."

Yes, he was Norse. He obsessed over Viking gods and *Valkyries.*

"You can't be a Valkyrie. They're beautiful women who reward fallen warriors."

He rolled his eyes. "That's so sexist. Why do Valkyries have to be women?"

She tried to laugh but it came out choked. "I'm not a warrior. I haven't done anything special."

"As you've said to me before, you work in the trenches. I've been studying those fighting the current battles of the education system to select the best to bring with me." He reached out a hand toward her.

Doris tried to shuffle forward to take his hand. Instead, she swayed and fell to her knees. The pain in her chest was greater than ever. She clutched at the front of her coat.

Erik rushed forward and caught her. "Mrs. Fairview, are you all right?"

"I'm having, think it's a, my . . . heart attack," she said. Her vision swam.

"How can you be having a heart attack?" He gasped. "Oh, no. You didn't eat the apple I gave you?" Tears filled Erik's eyes.

Doris understood her mistake. He hadn't been trying to poison her. He'd been trying to save her, only she hadn't been able to see what he offered. After all those years of teaching a thankless job, she'd been blind to anyone who might actually care about what she did. When someone had finally appreciated her hard work and wanted to reward her, she'd been too suspicious to see it. Frustration at her unworthiness washed over her in a suffocating tide. Her vision became a narrow tunnel.

She tried to speak, but she couldn't get out the words. She could feel her life draining away. "Didn't . . . pass . . . test."

"Or course you did." Erik reached into his pocket, a slow smile spreading over his face. "It's okay. I have another."

The world around them grew brighter. She had to squint to see him now. The pain in her chest faded away.

He held the apple out to her. "Do you want to be rewarded for your service?"

The apple glowed gold. She took it, noticing how it smelled

of autumn and her childhood. She could speak more easily now. "Thank you for the offer, but I don't want immortality. I don't want to teach second-graders for eternity. Nor would I enjoy Valhalla."

"No, of course not. You deserve some rest. That's why I'm offering you Freyja's hall."

As she bit in, she tasted golden light and freedom. She tasted cross word puzzles, hot tea and a warm fire. She tasted Folkvangr.

About the Author

SARINA DORIE has sold over 190 short stories to markets like Analog, Daily Science Fiction, Magazine of F & SF, and Orson Scott Card's IGMS. Her stories and published novels have won humor contests and Romance Writer of America awards. She has over eighty novels published, including her bestselling series, *Womby's School for Wayward Witches*. WRATH OF THE TOOTH FAIRY recently came out with Reuts Publishing.

A few of her favorite things include: gluten-free brownies (not necessarily glutton-free), Star Trek, steampunk aesthetics, fairies, Severus Snape, Captain Jack Sparrow, and Mr. Darcy.

By day, Sarina is a public-school art teacher, artist, belly dance performer and instructor, copy editor, fashion designer, event organizer and probably a few other things. By night, she writes. As you might imagine, this leaves little time for sleep.

You can find info about her short stories and novels on her website: **www.sarinadorie.com**.

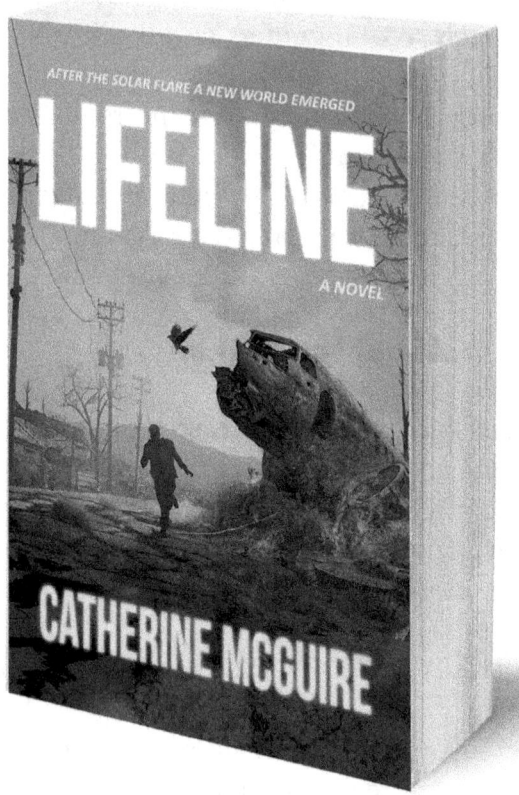

Fifty years after a massive solar flare ravages modern industrial civilization, a young man named Martin Barrister has a difficult job. He must attempt to e-establish communication links with the rest of the country. Yet, things aren't what they seem. The world outside New York City is very different and he may be caught up in a web of dangerous dealing and potential warfare.

Available in paperback and electronic editions.

The Monster Hunter

By Gregg Chamberlain

R ABBI SHULMAN, CAN I talk to you?"
Ezra Shulman looked up from his desk where he
was reviewing the accounts for the shul. Moishe
Cohen stood at the threshold of the rabbi's office door, one
foot stepping forward, the other hanging back. Like Cohen
himself, thought the rabbi, always half-in and half-out, one
side or the other, but very seldom on the mark.

Rabbi Shulman set a pen down between the pages of
the ledger to mark his place and closed the accounts book.
"Come in, Moishe," he gestured, sliding the ledger over,
out of the way, to one side of the desk. It didn't slide very
far. The desk was crowded with an old oversized computer
monitor and its tower drive/modem, along with various
books and folders and papers, diskettes and flashdrives.
More of the same, but without the diskettes and drives, sat
in piles around the office.

"Find a chair and sit down," the rabbi said to his visitor,
and waited, hands folded, for the other to get settled. "So,
Moishe, what can I do for you?"

Moishe Cohen sat quiet and fidgeted for a bit. A
small man, his neck craned so he could look up past
the rabbi at the wall while he gathered his thoughts. A
framed reproduction hung there, of an oil landscape of
Old Cabbagetown. Cohen then glanced left, then right,
then down at his twiddling fingers. Finally, he shrugged

his shoulders. "I need to ask you about something, Rebbe, something," he hesitated, "something maybe you might find hard to believe."

"Nu? So, ask." Rabbi Shulman resigned himself to not getting the shul accounts finished tonight. Not unless he took the ledger home with him and reviewed it during commercial breaks while watching the Stanley Cup playoffs. Leafs versus the Habs, just like in the old days. He sighed. It could be a classic, God willing.

Cohen started fidgeting again but forced himself to stop. "It's kind of complicated," he told the rabbi. "I'm not really sure where to start."

"At the beginning is always good," the rabbi suggested. "Is it maybe a personal problem?"

Cohen shook his head. "No, it's nothing personal, not really." He took a deep breath, like a diver preparing to take the plunge. "It's my neighbour."

Rabbi Shulman nodded. "Your neighbour? I see."

The other man nodded. "My next-door neighbour. Irving Nussbaum."

Lips pursed in thought, Rabbi Shulman said, "Nussbaum? I don't recall anyone by that name at temple."

Cohen nodded again, vigorously. "You're right. He doesn't go to temple. I'm sure of it."

"So it goes these days," the rabbi remarked, hands raised upwards in resignation. "Is this a problem for you, Moishe? You're not so regular yourself, you know."

The other man shook his head in fast, short jerks. "That's not it, rabbi. It's part of the problem, but it's not THE problem, y'understand?"

Lips still pursed, Rabbi Shulman slowly shook his own head. "No, I don't, actually." He looked over the rim of his glasses at Moishe Cohen. "Why don't you explain to me what the problem is."

The other man appeared to hesitate again. Another deep breath. Then he plunged ahead.

"I think Irving Nussbaum is a Vampire."

THE MICROWAVE BEEPED. Rabbi Shulman opened the door and took out two mugs of hot water. Dropping a tea bag into each mug, he carried them across the small office space, handed one over to Moishe Cohen, and set the other down on the little bit of open space on his desk. He took his time sitting down, lifting up his cup, cradling its warmth in his hands, smelling the aroma of the chamomile, then taking a cautious, careful, and slow sip.

Rabbi Shulman sighed. No Stanley Cup series tonight, he knew that for a fact. A whole hour he'd spent listening to Moishe Cohen explain his belief that Nussbaum, his neighbour, was a night-stalking nosferatu.

"His teeth! You should see them!" Moishe had lifted his lip with a finger, exposing one of his own bicuspids. "Like fangs they are!"

The rabbi took another long slow sip of his tea before setting the mug down. On the other side of the desk, Cohen perched on the edge of his chair, mug clutched in both hands, untasted and slowly cooling.

"So, rabbi, what do you think I should do?"

Rabbi Shulman's mouth opened, then closed. He sighed. Took another long, slow sip of tea. Thought a moment. Drank some more tea.

He could feel Cohen's eyes staring at him from the other side of the desk. Well, he thought, time to finish this meshuga. Maybe I can catch the third period.

"Tell me something, Moishe," he began, "you're not on any medications for anything, are you?"

The other man stiffened and stared. His mouth opened

and closed like a fish gulping air. "What," he gulped. "What are you saying, rabbi?"

Rabbi Shulman placed his hands flat on the desk around his mug of now-cold tea. "I'm saying—and don't take this the wrong way—I'm saying, Moishe, that maybe you might be letting your imagination get the better of you. That maybe you should get more sleep. That maybe you could do with a little holiday, like a nice visit out in the country or at the beach, maybe."

Cohen frowned. He set his mug on the desk. :"You don't believe me. You think I'm messhuganah."

The rabbi sighed, shrugged. "It's a crazy thing you're telling me, Moishe. Be honest, if I'd come to you with this story, what would you say?"

"But, Rebbe." Cohen leaned forward, gripping the edge of the desk. "He doesn't go to temple. Heavy curtains cover every window of his house. I've never seen him outside during the day, except maybe when there's a thick fog in the morning, and then only long enough to pick up his paper on the porch. He—"

"Maybe works nights, like lots of people do, so he sleeps during the day."

"There are no mirrors in his house, I swear to God, not one!"

Rabbi Shulman looked over the rim of his glasses at the other man. "And you know this...how?"

Cohen returned the rabbi's quizzical look with a defiant glare. "Maybe I was inside once...and looked around."

The rabbi frowned. "Moishe Cohen, you listen to me now—no, you will be silent and listen! Never mind that you've as good as said you broke into someone's house—I'm a rabbi, not a priest, and this is an office in Beth El shul, not a confessional booth over at St. Vincent's, but I still won't be going telling tales to the police." He held up a hand to silence the other's objection. "Not yet I won't, not unless you force me, and that means you sit and you listen and you think about what I'm saying to you. Moishe, this story you've told me, this cockamamie fantasy about your next-door neighbour is just simply the craziest thing I've ever heard. And I've listened to old Mrs. Klein telling me about how she sees Hitler come 'round to collect her blue box every recycling day Tuesday."

Again the admonishing hand lifted. "No, Not another word, Moishe. There are no such things as vampires. No ghosts and no ghouls, no dybbuks or doppelgangers. If you're not on medication and you're not drinking more than you should, and if this is not some silly joke, then you maybe need to start seeing someone who's more qualified than me to help you deal with your problem."

Moishe Cohen sat for a long moment and stared at Rabbi Shulman. Then, without a word, he stood up, turned, and stalked out of the office.

The rabbi shook his head and sighed. Sometimes sober and stern was the only best way. The results didn't always show up right off, but in the end, things worked out, more often than not. He hoped this would one of those times.

Sighing again, he reached over and dragged the accounts ledger back in front of him. Fingertips drummed on the cover for a moment. Then Rabbi Shulman flipped open the ledger to the page where he'd left the pen for a marker. A few more pages he promised himself, just so he could go home tonight knowing he'd managed to get something done.

MOISHE COHEN COULD not believe it. He left the shul and walked to the bus stop, feeling stunned, feeling disappointed, feeling just, well, not betrayed, but very, very hurt.

The rabbi didn't believe him, didn't believe what he had discovered about Irving Nussbaum. What is a man to do when even his own rabbi won't believe him? Even thinks he may be a little bit, well, crazy?

When the bus arrived, Moishe got on, swiped his fare card, and moved on down the aisle. He found an empty seat by a window near the rear exit doors. He stared out the window, not seeing the passing street scene, and thought to himself, *What do I do now?*

He knew he wasn't crazy, not even a little bit. It would be nice if he was, easier, in fact, if he was insane. But he wasn't, no sir, not at all. He knew what he knew. What he knew was his neighbour was a creature of the night, one of the undead. Nussbaum the vampire.

So what's to do? He wondered and he pondered. He examined the question from all sides, looked at it up, down and sideways. And, in the end, arrived at the obvious logical answer.

MOISHE COHEN'S HOUSE was at the end of a quiet cul-de-sac in a quiet neighbourhood not too far from Toronto's Kensington Market. Irving Nussbaum, his nosferatu neighbour, that bloodsucking shmo, lived—or maybe unlived was the proper term, maybe? Whatever. That putz of a parasite had his house to the left of Moishe's.

It was late in the afternoon when Moishe left the shul. As he arrived home the sun was more than halfway down the sky now, promising a pleasantly warm evening. The first full moon of early spring was also already easy to see above the horizon to the west. A pale round orb that would soon brighten the nighttime sky later.

Not that Nussbaum will see it, Moishe Cohen promised himself. No night-time hunting anymore for his bloodsucking neighbour. Not tonight or any other night ever again.

Inside his house, Moishe looked around for what he needed. But finding something that would serve as a stake wasn't as simple as he'd thought. Who bought much of anything made of wood anymore these days?

Well, there was the dining room table set. That could work. The table legs were nice and thick but they were fixed too solid for him to break off and he didn't have a saw. Moishe Cohen was no Mike Holmes Mr. Fix-It. One of the chairs then. With a bit of effort, and one sore right heel, after stomping repeatedly against one of the chairs he'd propped upside down on the floor,

Moishe had a couple of okay-looking stakes to sharpen. He managed that using a kitchen carving knife. The blade was likely pretty dull now but that didn't matter when there was a vampire to deal with.

Now for something to pound the stakes into Nussbaum's undead chest. Moishe considered the dining room table legs again then discarded that idea. He hunted around the house and then finally decided that maybe a kitchen rolling pin would work. Good thing his wife was away, visiting her mother. She'd never understand.

Okay, then, thought Moishe, I've got my rolling pin, I've got—he glanced out the window—still a good hour or more of daylight left. He smiled. Plenty of time before Nussbaum would rise from his coffin in search of unsuspecting virgins.

Moishe frowned in thought. Did vampires still sleep in coffins? And what is it with the virgins anyway? He shook his head. No time to waste pondering the mysterious ways of the undead. Moishe Cohen had vampire slaying to do.

He slipped out the back door. Caution was the watchword now. A man stepping out his front door, carrying a pair of sharpened stakes and a rolling pin might be seen and subjected to delaying, and difficult, questions. Worse still, someone might call the police, and wouldn't Nussbaum just love for that to happen. A vampire rescued from his Van Helsing by Toronto's finest.

Moishe took a quick look around his back yard. No one looking over a neighbouring fence, waving a friendly hello. Good. He scuttled to the gate that opened out to the back lane where everyone had their garbage cans and recycling bins set out already for tomorrow morning's pickup. He gave a fast look up and down the lane. No one. Closing his own gate, he skulked along the lane to the gate that led into Nussbaum's back yard.

With a quick look around, he first pressed gently against the gate. Finding it shut fast, he reached over the top to fumble around a bit before locating and lifting the latch.

The gate creaked as it opened. A loud creak, or so it seemed to Moishe's ears. He froze. Looked about. No house lights snapped on. No back doors banged open. No shouts of alarm. No "What do you think you're doing there?" Nothing. His hunched shoulders relaxed and Moishe smiled, pushing the gate open wide and entering Nussbaum's back yard.

He scurried across the yard to the back door. Which was locked, as he had expected, though he tried the knob just in case. No matter. He already knew how he was getting inside. Unless Nussbaum had discovered the weakness in his home security, which Moishe doubted.

Around a corner of the house Moishe crept, stopping at a basement window on the side of the house facing his own home. Something was wrong with the catch of this window because it remained unlocked. He'd discovered this one night when he'd gone prowling around Nussbaum's place, certain at the time that his neighbour was away and about a vampire's bloodthirsty business. With luck, the catch was still broken.

It was. Moishe slid the window slowly open and slipped inside Nussbaum's basement. He was a bit awkward about it this time because one hand and arm held the stakes and rolling pin clutched tight to his chest. But he managed in the end.

For a vampire, Moishe thought, Nussbaum had a very ordinary-looking basement. A rumbling oil furnace stood tucked away over in one corner. A couple piles of cardboard boxes sat against the far wall. A dusty workbench ran along another wall. But not a coffin in sight, which had surprised Moishe the first time he'd been inside Nussbaum's house. But then he figured maybe Nussbaum had his resting place tucked up inside some little attic-type space hidden underneath the roof. More private that way. Not to mention secure. Except where a determined vampire hunter like Moishe Cohen was concerned.

Moishe stole cautiously up the basement stairs. The door at the top was closed. He pressed an ear to it and listened. Not a sound. Slowly, he cracked open the door and peeped out.

Nothing but an ordinary kitchen. Fridge, stove, sinks and shelves. The window curtains—not the frilly, see-through ornamental sort, but a heavy cloaking kind—were drawn closed.

Moishe crept through the kitchen quietly and continued on throughout the house. All the rooms were dim because every window had the same heavy cloaking style of curtains drawn fast. He knew, from past outside observations, that all the larger windows also had regular window shades pulled all the way down during the daytime.

Living room, dining room, front hallway. Moishe searched quickly. Downstairs bathroom, back porch mud room, hall closet., and that little storage room under the stairs like in the Harry Potter movies. Moishe checked everything, swiftly, silently, all over the ground floor. Just to be sure, mind. Not that he expected to find Nussbaum in a recliner chair watching T.V. in the den or having a cup of tea in the kitchen.

He tried to creep up the stairs to the second floor but gave that up. Every step he planted a foot on creaked loud in his ears. Time was wasting anyways, so he trotted up the stairs, stake and rolling pin ready.

OISHE WAS SURPRISED to find Irving Nussbaum in the upstairs master bedroom. The room was dark, both because of the heavy window curtains drawn tightly closed and because it was getting darker outside now. Hardly any daylight glow at all seeped in above the top of the curtains. Moishe didn't have much time.

Nussbaum lay stretched out on top of the bed. His folded hands rested on his stomach. He was fully dressed, from his argyle socks and check slacks to his plaid cardigan. A fashion plate, he ain't, thought Moishe.

Softly, almost on tip-toe, Moishe stole up to the side of the bed. He tried to breathe slowly so as not to make any noise at all. He looked down at his target.

Irving Nussbaum didn't seem like much of a vampire, Moishe had to admit. Never mind his tasteless choice in clothes, Nussbaum just looked so...ordinary. With his pale, receding hairline, the slightly doughy face, and the pudgy physique, Irving Nussbaum more resembled a middle-aged office worker who spent too much time at his cubicle desk than a fearsome bloodsucking night-stalking lord of the undead. He looked more like Dracula's accountant, Nussbaum did.

But Moishe knew better. Not every man looked like an Arnold Schwarzenegger or a Denzel Washington. So why should every vampire look like a Lugosi or that kid in the *Twilight* movies?

No, all the facts fit. Moishe knew what he knew. Even now, he was sure he could see what looked like the pointed tip of a fang jutting out from beneath Nussbaum's upper lip.

He had to do it now, while there was still time. Swiftly, Moishe brought up one of his homemade stakes, positioned its tip just above, but not touching, Nussbaum's chest, and fumbled to get a tighter grip on his rolling pin without dropping it.

Was Nussbaum stirring? Were his twitching fingers looking more like claws? Were his lips showing just a little more fang now? Were those puffy eyelids fluttering just a bit before they would snap open, revealing bloodshot eyes blazing with an unholy light?

Now. It had to be now for Moishe. Now before it was too late. Now while he still had the strength of his conviction. Now!

The rolling pin swung down. Slammed against the top of the stake. The tip of the crudely-sharpened wood pierced the loudly-dyed fabric of the cardigan. Penetrated. Crimson blood spurted.

Irving Nussbaum roared. Moishe Cohen's rolling pin struck again. The stake pushed further down. Nussbaum lurched, deep growls rumbling from his parted lips, as he struggled to rise. Moishe staggered but kept hitting and hitting and hitting, the stake sliding deeper and deeper and deeper. Nussbaum stopped struggling and fell back still and silent now. Moishe kept swinging his rolling pin, hitting and hitting until there was a loud CRACK!

Half of the rolling pin flew away, landing with a muffled thump on the carpet on the opposite side of the bed. Moishe paused, gasping, blinking in surprise. He looked down.

Nussbaum's body lay pinned to the bed. The end of the stake, maybe as long as Moishe's hand, projected up out of the cardigan. A dark stain slowly spread out across the bedspread. There was no sign of life in Irving Nussbaum, not that a vampire was really alive, after all. It was over. Nussbaum the vampire was well and truly dead now. Moishe Cohen had saved the city from an unholy menace.

Moishe staggered back from the bed a step or two. He still

held the other half of the rolling pin in his hand. He looked down at it, willed his clenched fingers to open, and watched it fall to a thud on the floor. The other extra stake was still tucked like a sword under his belt. He left it there. Took one step forward, then another, until he stood by the bed again. He bent down for a closer look at the now-completely-dead Irving Nussbaum.

Funny how he still looked so ordinary. A bit fuzzier too in the dim light. And wasn't he supposed to be crumbling away into dust now? Oh, well, Moishe thought, maybe he was a young vampire and his body will now just go back to its natural process of decay.

Still, never hurts to be sure. Moishe had left his carving knife back in the kitchen after making his stakes. It was still likely too dull anyway. He didn't feel like hunting around Nussbaum's place for anything big enough to cut off the ex-vampire's head. But a good strong dose of morning sunlight would do the trick just as well. He strode around to the bedroom window, grabbed hold of the heavy curtain and, after a couple real hard yanks, managed to pull it down with a muffled clatter of the hanging rod. One end of rod tore a hole in the now-exposed window shade. Moishe finished the job. The big glass windowpane looked out upon the dusky skyline. Tomorrow's dawn would provide the finishing touch to Moishe Cohen's heroic deed.

Without a backward glance, Moishe left the bedroom. Down the stairs and through the house he went. To the back door. Not out through the basement window this time. No, a hero did not scuttle away from the scene of his triumph. Though a bit of discretion maybe would not go amiss even now. There was still no need to attract any unwanted official attention to himself. So it was out the back door and across Nussbaum's back yard in a few quick strides to the gate, out into the lane and then back inside his own house through his own back door. Moishe Cohen stood in his living room, safe and satisfied with his success.

Q UIT SHOVING," MOISHE mumbled, reaching behind to push away whoever was poking him in the ribs while he waited his chance to exit the bus. The poking continued, more insistent now.

Moishe made a quick grab and felt something hard and wooden in his hand. A splinter jabbed into a finger. He yelped. And woke up.

"Well, it's about time."

Moishe blinked and looked around. He was in the recliner chair in his own living room. Now he remembered. He'd sat down in the chair to take a little rest, as exhaustion took over from the adrenaline rush of his triumphant adventure over at Nussbaum's house.

Nussbaum. That voice he'd heard when he awoke. With a start his head snapped back around. He stared up at Irving Nussbaum glaring down at him.

Irving Nussbaum. Who was supposed to be dead for sure, but didn't look so much dead right now. Even with the hole in the middle of his chest which Moishe could see very clearly, thanks to the dark bloodstain marring the otherwise still-very-loud colours of the cardigan. Nussbaum still looked like an accountant, a very annoyed, even angry, accountant. His face twitched with what Moishe assumed was anger, or maybe outrage, fury, the whole megilla. One hand held the butt end of what the surprised vampire-slayer recognized as the homemade stake he'd last seen hammered into Nussbaum's chest. The pointed end of the stake, streaked with dark trails of dried blood, tapped tapped tapped against the open palm of Nussbaum's other hand.

Nussbaum continued to glare down at Moishe's fear-frozen face. "Would you maybe like to explain what you thought you were doing in my house?" The stake stopped tapping, its bloodstained tip rested in Nussbaum's still open hand. "Not that I don't appreciate the wake-up call, but a simple knock on the door and a 'Hey, Nussbaum! Time to get up!' would have been enough."

Moishe lifted a shaking finger. "Y-y-y-you're…you're not dead?"

The stake resumed tapping in Nussbaum's hand. "No, I am not dead," he growled, then smiled, a noticeable tic pulling at one corner of his mouth. "Not that you didn't give it a good…whack, so to speak. Took me a good hour or more to work that damn stake up far enough to clear the mattress so I could sit up." The stake tip shifted away and indicated a point a couple inches away from the hole in the cardigan. "But you missed the heart. Next time you should aim here."

Moishe blinked. "Next time?"

Nussbaum shrugged. "Well, maybe not." He grasped the stake with both hands in front of him, pointing it down towards the floor. "Of course, I have to kill you now." He shrugged again. "Tit for tat. Seems only fair after all. You know you've made me really late for my night watch detail at the mall. You think it's easy these days finding any kind of nighttime solo shift work? I can't afford to get laid off. Mall security pay's not great but it beats collecting UIC. Not sure what kind of excuse I can use. Getting stuck in traffic sure won't wash."

He looked thoughtful. "Maybe if I coughed a little bit, I could call in, claim some sick leave time, just for tonight. That stake of yours nicked a lung. Might make for a decent wheezing sound while the hole heals up."

Moishe wasn't listening. Nussbaum seemed distracted and he was taking advantage. He rolled over and off the recliner. Scrambling to his feet he positioned the recliner between himself and his unwelcome surprise visitor. *Unwelcome?*

"Hey, wait a minute," he exclaimed. "How did *you* get in *my* house? I didn't invite you!"

Nussbaum looked surprised. "Invite me? Oh, I get it now." He shook his head and smiled. "Right, right. The wooden stake, my bedroom window curtains pulled down to let the morning sunlight in. Sure. Now I understand."

Moishe watched as a hairy hand tossed away the useless wooden stake. He looked up to see a lupine smile spread across Nussbaum's face. Lips now gone black parted in a fang-filled grin.

"Oy," said the werewolf. "Did YOU get the wrong monster!"

Note: First published in Pulp Literature Magazine 10 (Spring, 2016)

About the Author

GREGG CHAMBERLAIN lives in rural Ontario, Canada, with his missus, Anne, and their two cats, who let the humans do all the mouse-catching in the house. He has two previous appearances in MYTHIC ("In Business to Protect and Serve", and "Jack's Lantern"). "The Monster Hunter" appeared in Pulp Literature Magazine in 2016, and is one of his favourite stories. The first draft was written,literally, while he was at home one autumn, half-listening to Coronation Street on CBC. Gregg writes speculative fiction for fun, and has several dozen published examples of his fun in venues that include: Abyss & Apex, Daily Science Fiction, Polar Borealis, Speculative North, Weirdbook, and other magazines, and various anthologies.

FEATURING ORIGINAL STORIES BY
GINI KOCH ● DEAN WESLEY SMITH ● NINA KIRIKI HOFFMAN
DAVID B. COE ● JOHN MICHAEL GREER ● ALEX SHVARTSMAN
KEVIN MCLAUGHLIN ● JOSHUA PALMATIER ● ANNIE REED
AND OTHERS!

SILENCE IN THE CITY

STORIES OF THE SUDDEN END OF THE MODERN WORLD

EDITED BY

SHAUN KILGORE

Sudden disruptions in power and other major services sends a city into chaos. In the blink of an eye, the modern technological world fails. Is it a government plot? Experiment gone wrong? A foreign cyber-attack? Alien invasion? A mystical incursion from beings beyond this dimension? Who knows? Now the noise and the bustle of the city has vanished, and an eerie silence settles over the urban landscape. Within, there are stories of human violence, depravity, an+d desperation, but also heroism, selflessness, and sacrifice. Silence in the City is an anthology of speculative tales asking what happens when a city—and all of modern civilization—is plunged into darkness.

Read great stories by Alex Shvartsman, David B. Coe, Joshua Palmatier, Gini Koch (writing as A.E. Stanton), D.A. D'Amico, John Michael Greer, Dean Wesley Smith, Nina Kiriki Hoffman, Kevin McLaughlin, Kirsten Cross, D.B. Keele, Annie Reed and Shaun Kilgore.

Through the Tulgey Wood

By Jon Gauthier

HE LATE-SUMMER AIR was heavy and wet, and it clutched a molasses-like quality that seemed to seep into her bones and impede every move she made. The headache that had plagued her since noon now thumped wildly at her skull. As she headed toward the stairs, a bright yellow mop of hair appeared. Molly, breached the top of the stair case and ran toward Ava, her arms outstretched.

"Mom!" Molly cried. Her voice was high and whiney. "Jemmyfroouffuggatme!"

Ava's instantly decoded the slurred babble and she shouted down the stairs, "Jeremy! Did you throw a frog at your sister?"

The stairs creaked and a dirty, freckle-streaked face appeared. Her son's hands were cupped together, forming an egg-shaped container that Ava knew held the aforementioned frog.

"Jeremy," Ava huffed. "You better not have brought that frog into the house!"

His gaze and shoulders immediately dropped.

"You bring it right back outside," Ava said, doing her best to keep the sternness to a minimum. "And make sure to wash your hands. It's almost lunch time."

Jeremy's lips formed a pout and he spun around with a sigh. As he stomped down the stairs in defeat, Molly danced behind him, gloating with singsong glee. Ava knew that they'd be screeching at each other again in less than a minute, but she took the opportunity to take in a deep breath and shift her mind back to the unpacking. There were still dozens of boxes scattered throughout the house, and it was clear the kids weren't going to be much help.

She moved down the hallway that separated the kids' rooms and looked out the window. From this vantage point, she could see the entire rear of the property: an acre of lush green grass dotted with well-kept maple, apple and spruce trees. The expanse unrolled into a pine forest that was so dense, Ava could only see a dozen feet into it. It was a beautiful and tranquil setting—the perfect place for her and the kids to start over.

The perfect place to keep Jeremy from having another episode.

"Mommy!" The screech snapped Ava out of her momentarily serene state of mind, and she let out a sigh.

"Molly!" she called wearily as she trudged down the stairs. "Leave you brother alone."

SLEEP WAS IMPOSSIBLE. The woodland symphony of crickets, frogs and God-only-knew what else was constant stream flowing through her open bedroom window. With the window closed, though, it would be far too hot— even at the tail end of August. Ava switched on her bedside lamp, opened the combination lock that was affixed to her nightstand drawer and pulled out a tattered paperback copy of Stephen King's *IT*. She'd been reading the book for more than a year, chipping away at it a dozen or so pages at a time.

She narrowed her eyes at the tiny print and wished she could have an e-reader like every else on the damned planet. It was too risky, though. If Jeremy ever got a hold of it he'd have access to any book he wanted—pictures and all. It was much safer this way, a paper brick full only with words he could barely understand and the cover torn off (that creepy cover with that green hand coming out of the sewer. Imagine if he'd seen that...) After only a few pages, Ava felt herself finally begin to drift off. She turned onto her side and let her eyelids become heavy as the words began to fuse together on the yellowed page like a swarm of black flies.

Then...

She's back at the old house and David is a mess of red and black pulp on the driveway, with a massive Bengal tiger standing in his remains, slurping up pieces of him like he's a bowl of Purina Fancy Feast. The tiger looks at her—its coat is so perfectly orange and black. It's like a drawing. And its teeth are diamonds dripping with gore. Fire in his eyes.

Fire!

She remembers. He's afraid of fire.

She bolts into the house and hears claws scraping the asphalt as it bounds after her. She flings the door closed and its bulk slams into the heavy wood. There's growling and scraping and she leaves it behind as she clambers into the kitchen.

Mommy!

Stay upstairs! Her voice is shrill—almost incomprehensible.

She tears open the junk drawer and rifles through the old pens and rubber bands until she finds a box of matches. She runs back to the main room just as the tiger explodes through the front door, the heavy oak splintering like balsa wood. With shaking hands she strikes a match against the box a moment before the beast pounces. She sees the reflection of the flame in its jagged porcelain maw and hears it shriek in fear before vanishing in a wisp of ghostly mist.

Mommy? The children are on the stairs. Molly is clutching one of her dolls and Jeremy is hugging a book to his chest. It's a large illustrated edition of "The Jungle Book." They'd been reading it together just before the tiger—before Shere Khan—appeared.

Mommy?

"Mommy?"

Ava's eyes snapped open to see a tiny face staring down at her. In a flurry of panic and muttered curses, she sat up and tore away her blankets, frantically looking for the copy of *IT.* She'd stupidly fallen asleep without locking it back in her nightstand. Ava lay flat and let her head hang just above the floor, her face pointed at the dark space beneath the bed. The book was there. She snatched it, flipped back up into a sitting position and quickly locked it back up in the nightstand where it would be safe from Jeremy and his... his...

Condition.

That's what it was, after all. A condition. Just a condition that they would all have to learn to live with. Like a peanut allergy or dyslexia, or ADHD... they all just had to adapt. Keep moving forward.

She'd told everyone that it had been a bear—a crazed black bear that had just wandered into the neighborhood and attacked David while he was washing the minivan. Then it burst through the door and she scared it away by banging some pots together. And everyone had believed her. There had been no other possible explanation. And if she'd actually tried to give one? If she'd actually attempted to explain what really happened... that Jeremy had somehow--

"Mommy?" Ava's looked at Molly who cowering against the wall, staring at her mother with wide blue eyes and chewing anxiously on her fingers. Ava sighed and silently cursed at herself for scaring the girl.

"What is it, sweetie?" She tried to make her voice as soft as possible.

"Can I sleep with you?"

Ava looked at her bedside clock to see it was just past

3AM. She flopped back down on the mattress with a sigh and scooted over.

"Come on," she said.

Molly immediately hopped into the bed and nuzzled her face into her mother's shoulder. Ava switched off the bedside light and asked, "Did you have a nightmare?" She felt Molly's head shake out a 'no'.

"Are you just scared of the new house?"

Molly lifted her face and whispered, "There's a monster in the woods."

"Sweetie, you know there's no such thing as monsters." *A lie*, she thought. *Such a tremendous lie.*

"I swear, mommy. I heard it breaking branches and I looked out my window and saw it running away."

"What did it look like?"

"It was like a dragon," Molly said, he voice almost inaudibly quiet. "With a... with a fish head. And rabbit teeth."

Ava kissed the top of Molly's head and ran her fingers through her hair, something that always put her to sleep. Being two years older than Jeremy, Molly had seen plenty of books and movies and pictures before the "Jungle Book" incident. She would have been very familiar with dragons and any number of strange creatures.

"That sounds like a pretty silly monster to me," Ava said. Her daughter just giggled nervously in response before finally closing her eyes. Within minutes, they were both asleep.

THE NEXT MORNING, Molly seemed to be in good spirits and she happily ate her cereal. She didn't even put up much of a fuss whenever Jeremy did something to annoy her. Ava figured she'd forgotten all about her bad dream. Surely the monster—the dragon with the fish head and rabbit teeth—had only been part of a dream.

After breakfast, Ava shooed the kids outside and told them not to come back into the house until she called them for lunch. Now able to focus her attention on finishing the unpacking, she trudged up the stairs into Molly's bedroom. The floor was littered with partially unpacked boxes and the bed was awry with a pink and white tangle of sheets and blankets spilled halfway to the floor. Next to it stood an empty dresser and bookshelf.

Ava lifted one of the open boxes and dropped it onto the bed. As she started removing the various clothes that had been packed inside, she heard a single stinging scream come from the back yard. She rushed to the window and looked down to see Jeremy chasing Molly with a water gun. Ava rolled her eyes and turned back to the bed. Usually she could discern the kids' playful screams from the real ones. Maybe she was too anxious. She turned the box over and let all the clothes tumble to the bed.

It had taken less than an hour to finish with Molly's room. Of course, it would have gone quicker if she hadn't had to shout at the kids every ten minutes. When she walked into Jeremy's room, she was pleasantly surprised to see most of the unpacking had been done. He'd pretty much done everything expect hang up his button-up shirts.

Ava grabbed the shirts in a single bunch and walked over to the tiny closet. As she hung each garment, she noticed that a portion of the wood paneling seemed to stick out from the rest of the wall. The protuberance sloped diagonally for about two feet before becoming flush with the wall again. It took Ava a moment to realize what she was looking at. It was a door. A tiny trap door was built into the back of the closet. A sudden childlike sense of wonder and excitement took hold as she knelt in front of it. She was sure she had looked through the whole house before letting the kids inside yesterday, and she hadn't noticed this. Jeremy must have found it at some point and already looked inside. Ava reached for the door when another scream erupted from the yard. She could tell this one was real.

She didn't even bother going to the window. Instead she raced out of the room and down the stairs just in time to see the kids burst through the front door, both of them sweaty and red-faced.

They screamed in unison, "Mommy!"

Ava knelt down and embraced them. They were both hot and their hearts were pounding. She released them and put a hand on Molly's right shoulder and Jeremy's left. "What's going on? What are you two getting up to out there?"

"We saw the monster," Molly exclaimed breathlessly.

"Molly," Ava said. "Don't scare your brother. We talked about this last night. Monsters aren't real."

A lie. Such a lie, and you know it.

"No, Mommy," Molly said, stamping her foot. "We saw it in the woods."

"I sawed it too," Jeremy said. "It was like a big snake with legs."

"Jeremy!" She said it too loudly. Too sharply. Ava took in a deep breath and pulled him in close.

"There's no such thing as monsters," she said softly. "Your sister is just trying to scare you." Ava looked over at Molly with a piercing anger that only a mother is capable of conveying. "Now, I want both of you to stay apart for the rest of the morning," She said. "Molly, you can go and play in your room. Jeremy, you go and practice." She pointed to the living room where she'd set up Jeremy's electric keyboard.

"We're not lying," Molly said quietly. And as she and Jeremy stalked away to separate corners of the house, Ava realized that she believed her.

WHERE IN THE Hell did I put you," Ava muttered as she dug through the large plastic tote that sat at the back of the garage. She was looking for the desktop fan that she usually kept on her nightstand, unwilling to spend another night with the window open and those godforsaken critters keeping her awake. On her way back to the house, Ava stopped to take a long, more detailed look at the backyard. It was gorgeous at this time of day—just moments before sunset, the sky a watercolor painting hanging overhead the silent forest.

Ava wandered over to one of the apple trees and saw that it bore healthy-looking Mackintoshes that would be perfect for baking. She reached out and plucked one. It was something she hadn't done since she'd visited her grandparent's farm as a girl. She reveled in the simplicity and wholesomeness of it.

Then she heard something snap. It had come from the forest. It was followed by another snap. Then another. They came in a steady rhythm, like something was moving through the trees.

Ava took a single step toward the pines, surprised at how scared she'd suddenly become. At this time of day, it was probably just a deer or a moose. Not much else could make that much noise other than a bear, and the real estate agent had assured her that there hadn't been a bear spotted in this township for almost fifteen years.

She was about to take another step forward when a guttural clicking noise emerged from the thicket. It was like the sound of someone chocking and snapping their teeth together at the same time. It wasn't like anything Ava had ever heard before. It was so foreign—almost otherworldly—and it filled her with a near paralyzing sense of dread. She turned and dashed toward the house with a speed she didn't even know she was capable of.

Once inside, Ava set the fan on the floor, pulled the phone from its base on the counter, and dialed the number for the local police, thankful that she'd programmed into the phone's speedial on their first night in the house.

"It's just a deer," she said. "It's just a deer."

Is it, though? What if it's happening again?

"There are no pictures in this house," Ava said defiantly.

A woman answered, her voice deep and weary: "Police."

"Yes. Hi. Um... I'm sorry. I don't know if I should really be calling you..."

"Are you in danger, ma'am? Is this an emergency?"

"No. No. Nothing like that. It's just... I live out on Tremblay Road, and I heard a strange noise in the woods behind my house. Some kind of animal. I think it may be injured or... maybe rabid or something."

"Did you see the animal, ma'am?" The woman's sounded bored—almost annoyed.

"No, I just heard it. It made this really strange sound. I've never heard anything—"

"You can contact the municipal office in the morning," the woman said. "They'll send an animal control team to investigate." Ava could tell the woman had moved the phone away from her mouth as she was speaking. She was getting ready to hang up.

"It's just..." Ava said.

"It's just what, ma'am?"

"Well, we just moved here. Me and my children... and they... well, they thought they saw something in the woods this morning."

"Ma'am there's all sorts of things around here. Now, I'm not doubting you heard something. But unless you've actually seen the animal and believe it's a danger to you or someone else, you'll have to wait for animal control."

"I understand," Ava said, her face now hot with embarrassment. "I'm sorry. Thank you." She disconnected the call and set the phone on the counter.

"Don't do this," Ava whispered. "Keep it together."

Suddenly, the sliding door exploded into a shower of glass and a thick and scaly length of dark grey rubber shot into the kitchen. Ava screamed and dropped to the floor. She scrambled backward, staring at the intruding object as it thrashed about, snapping furiously in every possible direction as if searching for something.

Then Ava realized it wasn't rubber, but flesh.

It was a tail.

She rolled onto her knees and scrambled out of the kitchen just as a nightmarish shriek filled the entire house.

Ava charged upstairs. Jeremy and Molly were huddled next to one another on the landing.

"It's the monster!" Molly cried. "The monster, Mommy!"

"In my bedroom!" Ava screamed as she reached the top of the stairs. She shoved the kids forward and the three of them rushed into the master bedroom and slammed the door closed.

The shrieking continued, but Ava could tell that it was coming from outside now. Luckily the thing—whatever it was that the tail belonged to—didn't actually come into the house.

That means it's too big to get through the door. Ava pushed the thought away. She had to know what she was dealing with.

"You two get under the bed!"

The kids nodded and crawled beneath the bed as Ava crept to the window. Unlike the kids, her bedroom didn't overlook the backyard, but the front. She couldn't see anything but a lone oak tree and the gravel lane way that led to the pitch black road.

What in the Hell is it?

"They said it was a dragon," Ava said quietly.

No, they said it was like *a dragon. It's actually something different.*

Ava turned toward the bed and dropped to her knees. She grabbed her son's hand.

"Jeremy, where is the picture?"

He didn't answer.

"Jeremy, I know you saw a picture. Where did you see it? Did Molly draw it?"

Jeremy shook his head.

"Was it a book?"

He nodded.

"Where? Where is it?"

"My closet," he said quietly.

Ava suddenly remembered the small door she had seen in the back of Jeremy's closet.

"You two stay here," she said. "You do not move from this spot."

The kids nodded and Ava darted out of the bedroom and down the hall. She crashed through Jeremy's bedroom door, almost ripping it off the frame, and ran to the closet where she tore open the small trap door.

She got on her knees and stuck her head into a tiny room that was only about two feet high, wide, and deep. Inside were an old couch cushion and a small assortment of dolls and stuffed animals. None of the items belonged to her or the kids. It must have all been left behind by the previous owners. Ava moved the objects around until she finally found what she was looking for: a thin and tattered hardback book without a dust jacket.

She grabbed the book and flipped it over to see the title laid out in heavy black font: "Through the Looking Glass and What Alice Saw There."

Ava opened the book and flipped madly through the pages. She stopped when she landed on a black and white illustration of a small light-haired girl—Alice—kneeling on a mantle and looking into a mirror. She continued flipping, passing by horses and chess pieces before finally landing at her destination. The terrifying image stared back at her. It was of a small human figure standing in a dark forest with a massive sword raised above their head, facing down an almost indescribable creature. The monster was a long and serpentine thing with leathery wings and gnarled talons. Its face was an unearthly mishmash of buck teeth, blank eyes and spindly whiskers.

Ava's insides went to liquid when she saw the thing's tail. It was identical to the one that had smashed through the sliding door. This was it. This was what Jeremy had…

…summoned.

She tore her eyes from the drawing and looked at the text it accompanied. It seemed to a be a poem. The first line, "Beware the Jabberwock, my son!" was all she needed to read.

Ava ripped the page from the book just as something heavy landed on the roof. The noise thundered through the house, rattling the walls. There was another horrible shriek and the sound of a claws dragging across the shingles

The kids were still under the bed, and Ava heard them cry out in fear as she tumbled back into her bedroom. Above them, the unmistakable sound of splintering wood and falling debris was intermixed with that guttural clicking that Ava had heard when she was outside. The Jabberwock was tearing away the roof.

Ava looked down at the page and scanned poem, squinting at its many nonsensical words. Finally, she saw the ones she'd been looking for: "vorpal blade", "dead", and "head". She looked back at the person in the picture—at the sword in their hands. Then Ava dropped to her stomach and held the page out to Jeremy, her hands shaking.

"The sword, Jeremy!" She had to scream to be heard over the carnage above. "Bring the sword!"

Jeremy stared at her with wide uncomprehending eyes. He had no idea what she meant. He didn't even know what he could do—what he had done.

"The sword!" Ava screamed again, shaking the picture in front of his face. "Bring the sword just like you brought the monster. You can do it, sweetie. You know you can."

There was a crash as something landed on the attic floor. It sounded like it was above Molly's room. They didn't have much time left.

"Come on, Jeremy!" Ava cried. "I need you to be really brave, now. I need to close your eyes and think really hard about this sword, OK."

Jeremy's nodded and squeezed his eyelids together.

"That's it, sweety," Ava said. "Just think of the sword. Bring the sword."

The Jabberwock let out another shriek as it pounded and slashed at the attic floor.

"Jeremy," Ava moaned. "Jeremy, hurry."

Jeremy's eyes suddenly snapped open and he said, "It's on the bed now, mommy."

Ava got to her feet and saw a massive sword lying on her bed. It was at least 12 inches wide and took up almost the entire six foot length of the mattress. Ava's heart fell. There was no way she'd be able to lift.

One of the Jabberwock's front paws suddenly burst through the ceiling and Ava had to duck away from the razor talons. Without thinking, she grabbed the sword's hilt and swung it upwards. It was much lighter and the movement was much swifter than she had anticipated. She managed to nick the paw just as the Jabberwock pulled it back up into the attic. A thin spray of blood spattered Ava's face. There was a furious cry of pain and the clatter of claws on wood.

Sword at the ready, Ava stood firm, staring up at the hole in the ceiling and poised for the next attack. The Jabberwock's face appeared, bringing with it a hideous moaning snarl. Teeth the size of piano keys snapped at her and hot swamp-smelling saliva sprayed her face. The creature's eyes were beyond white, but seemed to focus on her regardless. Two antennae jutted from its head like giant spider legs. Ava swung at the monstrous face, barely missing it each time. It snapped its jaws at her in return, weaving forward and backward and side to side as it calculated the best moment to attack. The cat and mouse game went on for only a few seconds, but Ava's arms screamed with exhaustion. Finally—mercifully—she tore a deep gash into the Jabberwock's cheek. It let out a screeched and disappeared back through the hole.

Adrenaline coursed through Ava like an electric shock and she ran out of the bedroom, pulled open the hatch that led to the attic, and clambered up the ladder. Her head entered the attic just in time to see the Jabberwock's tail flick up through the opening it had torn into wall and roof.

Dragging the sword on the floor behind her, Ava jogged to the massive fissure. Snapped pieces of lumber stuck out like crooked teeth, making a crude ladder. She took hold of one of rungs and hoisted herself up. The climb was short but precarious, the twenty five-foot drop to the outside ground only a single mistake or broken board away.

It was waiting for her on the roof. Its hulking dragon-like form looked completely surreal against a backdrop of star-streak sky. Wasting no time, Ava drew up the sword and charged forward. The Jabberwock, seemingly surprised by her boldness, jerked backwards, its front paws clattering on the rooftop as it tried to re-position itself.

Ava thrust the sword forward. She swung it in every conceivable direction, fending off the swiping paws and snapping jaws as she ripped and tore at the monster's flesh. Then, seeming to gather all of its strength for a final attack, Jabberwock lowered its head and lunged forward, its hideous mouth wide and glistening. Ava stepped out of the way at the last possible moment and, with a final desperate snicker-snack, she chopped downward and sliced off the bottom half of the creature's jaw. It screeched and fell forward onto the roof and Ava brought the massive vorpal blade down on its neck. She struck it again and again, chopping away at the thick flesh until she finally felt it go through straight into the roof itself.

In the next moment, the Jabberwock's head was rolling away from her, vanishing just before it reached the edge of the roof. Ava felt a tremendous weight leave her hands and she looked down to the sword was gone to. Next to her, the Jabberwock's wings gave a final twitch before the entire corpse disappeared.

Ava was suddenly alone, the late August chill biting at her hot blood-stained skin. She looked out over the back yard and examined the deep dark woods where the thing had come from—where Jeremy had brought it from. *It will never end*, she thought. *He'll never be able to stop.* Dropping her head, Ava turned to the destroyed portion of roof that led down into her home, and went gallumping back.

I 'VE ONLY GOT half an hour for my lunch break," Ava said.

The man took the picture from her. "It's just a sketch, right?"

Ava nodded. "But his whole body," she said. "And it needs to look as much like him as possible."

He started thoughtfully at the picture for a moment and said, "I don't get it. I mean, I'm happy to take your money, but I don't get it. Why do you want a drawing of a photo?"

"It has to be a drawing," Ava responded. "It won't work otherwise."

"Ok," the man said, pointing at a sofa that sat at the

other end of the studio. "Just take a seat over there. It shouldn't take long."

Ava watched as he walked over to his desk, the photograph of her dead husband clutched between his thumb and index finger. Then she walked over to the couch and sat down.

And she waited.

Note: First published online at Tell-Tale Press (2019)

About the Author

Jon Gauthier is a horror and science fiction author whose work has appeared in multiple digital and print publications. He lives in Ottawa, Ontario, Canada with his wife and daughter. He can be found lurking on Twitter at @JAGaut.

Journey Star
By John Michael Greer

Reviewed by Frank Kaminski

Journey Star, 259 pp.
Founders House Publishing, 12/2021
Paperback, $15.99
eBook edition, $5.99.

JOHN MICHAEL GREER'S new novel *Journey Star*, like his other fiction to date, delightfully resists categorization. It is simultaneously a work of climate fiction, a first contact story, a space-faring adven-ture and an all-around epic piece of entertainment. It revels in classic science fiction themes and tropes while also building on them in brilliant ways. And it deals with challenging questions such as how best to manage potentially harmful technologies, and whether the redemption of humanity's home world would be worth pursuing even if its pursuit could lead us down a tyrannical path.

The book is a sequel to Greer's equally accomplished 2009 novel *The Fires of Shalsha* (which, incidentally, was his first novel, originally written in 1985-86). Both books depict a future in which Earth has been made uninhabitable by runaway climate change, and humans now inhabit about a dozen colony worlds spread out over numerous solar systems. Some of these colonies have managed to keep in touch by virtue of having a shared solar system, though this doesn't appear to be the norm. It seems most colonies are located in different systems, meaning that due to the difficulties involved in crossing the voids of interstellar space, they've had no contact with one another over their entire histories thus far. They're as isolated as a dozen salt grains scattered across a continent.

Our setting in both novels is Epsilon Eridani II, commonly known as Eridan. It's a world of abundant mineral resources, meadows of violet-colored moss, 600-foot-tall blue-leaved trees and primitive invertebrate creatures reminiscent of Earth's earliest land animals. Eridan's human society is unlike any before it on either Earth or Eridan. In its traditions, symbols, dress, cuisine and many other areas, it is heavily influenced by Japanese medieval society. Yet no one on Eridan speaks Japanese, or for that matter any of the other ancient languages of Earth. Nor is Eridan's technology limited to that of medieval Japan; it also includes an assortment of technologies from our own time as well as some entirely new technologies that are mental in nature (more on these later).

Human settlement on Eridan is constrained by the incompatibility of the planet's biochemistry with human nutritional needs. Eridan's fauna is non-amino acid-based and thus produces no protein. Most of its flora is likewise of no nutritional value to humans. Consequently, most of Eridan's human denizens subsist on vat-grown meat and hydroponic vegetables. These are grown in self-sufficient, renewably powered, concrete structures called Shelters, each of which houses several thousand people. Residents of these Shelters are known as "Shelter folk." Outside the Shelters lives a race of tribal nomads called the outrunners, who are forced to prey on both Shelter folk and one another. The protectors of the Shelter folk are an elite order of mystic warriors called the Halka. The Halka are like samurai who carry guns and grenades instead of katanas.

Journey Star is the name of the ship that brought humans to Eridan. The trip took multiple human lifetimes, and it has now been an additional three centuries since *Journey Star*'s crew made landfall and began settling the planet. Sixteen years into its history, Eridanian society was taken over by a totalitarian regime known as the Planetary Directorate, which was determined to reestablish an industrial base on Eridan as quickly as possible, no matter the human cost. Thus, the Directorate's reign saw millions die in slave labor camps while the rest of the populace suffered famine, poverty and mass-casualty drone strikes. This murderous regime was toppled by insurgents who used one of the Directorate's own nuclear weapons to take out its capital city of Shalsha.

That was more than two centuries ago. Since then, life on Eridan has been governed by a strict set of rules called the Six Laws, which forbid, among other things, violence, weapons of mass destruction, communities of more than 10,000, social hierarchies and damage to planetary or regional ecologies. These laws have made people highly selective in their use of early-21st-century technologies. Internal combustion engines, for example, are used only minimally and weapons are limited to a maximum effective range of one kilometer. The Six Laws have also brought Eridan a degree of peace and freedom previously unheard of throughout the entirety of human history. They are enforced by the Halka and are punishable by death.

In the previous novel, Eridan's long peace was broken by an attempted revival of banned Directorate-era technology. This new novel takes place two decades after that conflict. It begins with the Halka having eliminated the other main threat against human life on Eridan—namely, the outrunners, who have now all been driven to either extinction or assimilation. This creates a dilemma for the Halka: How can they remain relevant when their services as protectors are no longer needed? As if this quandary weren't enough, the Halka, along with the rest of Eridan's people, soon find themselves questioning their entire place in the universe with the discovery of a troubling space anomaly. In short, Eridan now finds itself at multiple historic crossroads, the implications of which are engagingly explored in *Journey Star*.

Greer is a masterful world builder, and this world is so believable and fully realized that I felt as if I were inhabiting it along with the characters. I especially appreciate Greer's attempts to offer plausible scientific rationalizations for the stark differences between Eridan's biology and ecology and those of present-day Earth. In explaining why Eridan's plant life is blue and purple rather than green, for instance, he draws on the real-life science of photosynthetic pigments. His explanation for why Eridan's fauna lacks protein is equally compelling. Moreover, the very fact that humans are unable to live off the land on Eridan without resorting to cannibalism is entirely grounded in real-world ecology. It illustrates the folly of expecting to be able to thrive in an ecology other than the one in which one's species evolved to thrive.

Not everything about Eridan is grounded in modern mainstream science; some of the planet's features are beyond our ken as early-21st-century Earthlings. A case in point is the dwimmerroot, a rootstalk that confers psychic powers on those who ingest it. (This is where the aforementioned mental technologies come into play.) Thanks to the mind-altering properties of dwimmerroot, members of the Halka order—who consume the root as an initiation rite—are able to mentally confer with one another by joining their minds into a single "groupmind." They can also instantaneously transmit minutes' worth of thoughts or instructions from mind to mind. Dwimmerroot leads some to have psychic visions, and others to become "mindhealers" capable of using their minds to rid others' of psychological trauma. The depth of detail with which these mental technologies are imagined and described transcends any need for a scientific explanation.

One of the great virtues of this story is its moral ambiguity. It has no heroes or villains, really, and the two groups we were most inclined to regard as villains in the last book—the outrunners and the Directorate—are shown in this one to be worthy of our sympathy, or at least our understanding. The outrunners preyed on Shelter folk because it was that or starve. The Directorate's leaders chose the path they did because their psychic visions showed them that every alternative was even bleaker. On the flip side, it turns out the Halka's status as a force for good is more problematic than it initially might have seemed. Nowhere to be found in this story are the obvious good-guys-versus-bad-guys scenarios of lesser novels. Instead, we're a little on everyone's side.

Journey Star's main characters are all well developed, but the two standouts are an orphaned outrunner girl named Asha and the Halka woman who adopts her, Carla Dubrenden sen Halka. As the last surviving member of Eridan's last free band of outrunners, Asha is grieving the loss of her former companions and way of life, while also struggling to find her place in a new world that is utterly foreign to her. Even though Carla was directly involved in the assault that left Asha without a family, Asha is philosophical about what happened and doesn't blame

Carla. But Carla feels a need to atone. A touching bond develops between these two, with Carla caring for Asha at first and then Asha doing the same for Carla as the need arises. As their private drama unfolds, we also watch two wildly divergent cultures come together and enrich each other.

Shalsha and *Journey Star* are significant departures from Greer's typical science fiction (aka "sf") writing. In the worlds of his other sf novels and stories, the hard sf narrative devices on which the present tales depend (interstellar travel, geoengineering, the colonization of other worlds) are impossible. *Star's Reach*, for example, is about accepting that humankind's dream of one day visiting or being visited by intelligent extraterrestrial life is most likely a fantasy. (The interstellar distances are just too great for either us or the aliens to have a realistic chance of bridging them.) In short, Greer's other sf is literally of a more down-to-earth variety; to quote a phrase he often uses, it deals in "the kind of futures we're actually likely to get." As much as I admire this more realistic brand of sf, I also love seeing Greer stretch himself into the weird and wonderful "what if" territory of golden age sf.

You don't need to have read *Shalsha* to follow *Journey Star*, as the new book tells its own self-contained tale and fills in newcomers on much of the first book's lore and storyline. As for the new story, the only other thing I'll give away is that it abounds in adventure, spy thriller-like intrigue, thought-provoking legal and moral debates, satisfying answers to a number of the first book's burning mysteries and the stunning moments of conceptual breakthrough for which great sf has long been known. The net effect is a novel that succeeds in recapturing the original's essence while also taking it in absorbing new directions.

Son of the Storm
By Suyi Davies Okungbowa

Reviewed by Kieran Judge

Son of the Storm, 450 pp.
Orbit, 5/2021
Paperback, $17.99
ebook, $4.99
Rating: 3/5

HIGH FANTASY HAS an issue, in that much of what is written still follows in the tradition of Tolkien and Lewis, who were very British and very white. Don't get me wrong; we love some medieval castle sieges, and there's stuff that goes against these stereotypes, but there's an awful lot less of it in the public consciousness and staring out at you as you walk into the bookshops than there could be (or at least there is for me in the UK).

How refreshing it is then to pick up *Son of the Storm*, a novel by a writer who grew up in Benin City, Nigeria, and features a world set in a fantasy world inspired and influenced by African traditions, beliefs, and cultures. The first entry in *The Nameless Republic Trilogy*, we follow Danso, a young scholar at the fringes of acceptance in the capital city of Bassa due to his mixed heritage, and Esheme, his betrothed, daughter of a powerful and influential city figure. When an assassin appears from a land of myth and legend, Danso is forced to go on the run through the land of Oon, whilst Esheme finds herself thrust into the position as head of her family, using her political influence to enact revolution on the streets of the capital.

The novel takes its time to set up the complexities of Bassa and its history. From the beginning, the traditions of the people are established, their belief that Bassa is the pillar of all that is good, and also the racial inequality present in Bassa. Okungbowa makes sure to make this one of the central thematic focuses of the novel, and manages to explore it through multiple aspects, from main hero Danso, to the character of Lilong, traveller from country afar.

There's an interesting magic system introduced in the novel in the drawing upon the power of a stone known as ibor, with different co-lours doing different things. We only really get shown red ibor in this novel, with promises of more to come in the second instalment, but it's fun to see a kind of environmentally-orientated power, as opposed to the 'believe in yourself and find your true magic' stuff we get so often.

The most interesting plotline in the novel is Esheme's growth from child to household leader to revolutionary. Delving into the underground politics of the city, the ordinary people, and watching her navigate it all, is fascinating. There's something about watching someone forced to become utterly ruthless which is compelling, and it's an arc with a myriad of questions to it. How far does one go before fighting for a correct cause becomes undermined by personal interests in power? Can the two ever exist side by side? Is power, even for a 'good' character, a good end result?

But unfortunately much of what makes the novel interesting or unique are the superficial changes to aesthetics that we've seen and read hundreds of times before. The actual storyline in itself is fairly generic and bog-standard; an obvious setup for the next instalment in the series, even with Esheme's arc. This couldn't exist as a standalone novel, and to a certain extent parts fall down as a result. With 40 pages to the end, we haven't even had our finale properly set up yet, though we're fairly sure of the kind of thing it will be; it feels like an afterthought. There's far more time and effort spent sitting around in other sections than our big climax here, and it feels like such a letdown, such an afterthought, that you leave disappointed.

This leads to my thinking that the novel could do with either 50 pages more, most of it in the later stages, or 50 pages less, to make it really work. If you add 50, you can properly flesh out this finale, instead of skipping over several days in the space of paragraphs leading to the final scenes. If you take out 50 pages, you can re-work the large paragraphs of exposition which have crept into the final draft into the narrative and, for example, have someone witness the different pidgin languages which are apparently spoken all throughout the lower parts of Bassa but never seen, rather than just saying that they speak it. Some of the large sections devoted to spelling out themes of racial inequality and environmental disaster could have been reworked naturally into the storyline in order to keep it flowing. Don't get me wrong; sometimes you need large sections to explain why a culture has grown up to be racially unequal, or have this historical tradition, or how people don't recognise the encroach of desertification onto their lands, and it sometimes needs to be on-the-nose because it's impossible to do otherwise. But there comes a point when it's starting to get in the way of buckling down and getting on with the story, and it grates.

Son of the Storm is a decent novel. It's got an interesting world, fun characters, and a slew of other unique elements to it. But there's also a lack of sharpness to it, a fairly familiar feel to the characters and the way the narrative develops, and not much which makes it stand out from a story perspective. It's got no surprises and, to a certain extent, does what you expect, for better or worse.

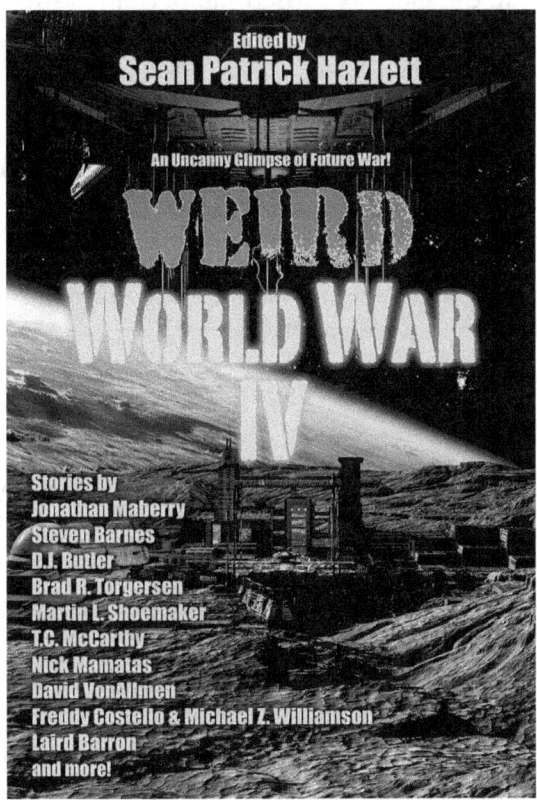

PATREON

Become A Patron Today!

If you haven't yet, please consider subscribing by becoming a Patron through **MYTHIC's Patreon Page.** Visit this address for more information: **www.patreon.com/mythicmag.** There are multiple ways to get monthly subscriptions. Help me keep MYTHIC going strong and growing into a top short fiction market.

INTERESTED IN SUBMITTING YOUR STORIES TO MYTHIC?

MYTHIC is looking for diverse science fiction and fantasy stories. You can send your submissions to me at <u>submissions@mythicmag.com</u>. Visit **www.mythicmag.com** for more information and instructions on how to format your submissions emails.

If you have any others questions, you can use the contact form on the website.

Advertise in MYTHIC

Do you have a science fiction or fantasy novel or anthology you'd like to promote? Consider advertising in MYTHIC. Please send all advertising inquires to mythicmag@gmail.com.

Here are our current rates:

Full-page: $100.00 per issue
Half-Page: $50.00 per issue
Quarter-page: $25.00 per issue
Back Cover: $150.00 per issue

COMING NEXT MONTH

ISSUE 20   MARCH 2022

MYTHIC

A SCIENCE FICTION & FANTASY MAGAZINE

FEATURING STORIES BY
MARK BILSBOROUGH | SEAN PATRICK HAZLETT
AARON EMMEL | WARREN BENEDETTO | AND MORE!
EDITED BY SHAUN KILGORE